Lock Down Publications and Ca$h
Presents

I0664786

THE
Dirty Side Of
MONEY 3
Hell To Pay

Written By
PRINCE
The Obsessive Gritty and Raw Urban/Street Crime Author

First Edition 2025

Printed in the United States of America

This is a work of fiction. Names, characters, places, and incidents either are products of the author's imagination or are used fictitiously. Any similarity to actual events or locales or persons, living or dead, is entirely coincidental.

Lock Down Publications
P.O. Box 944
Stockbridge, GA 30281
www.lockdownpublications.com

Like our page on Facebook: Lock Down Publications
www.facebook.com/lockdownpublications.ldp

Stay Connected with Us!

Text **LOCKDOWN** to 22828 to stay up-to-date with new releases, sneak peaks, contests and more…

Like our page on Facebook:
Lock Down Publications

Join Lock Down Publications/The New Era Reading Group

Visit our website:
www.lockdownpublications.com

Follow us on Instagram:
Lock Down Publications

Email Us: We want to hear from you!

AUTHOR'S NOTE

To my readers, both day-ones and those just now tapping in. I want to thank you for choosing to enter the worlds I create. Worlds that are dark, gritty, raw, and unflinching in their realism. I don't sugarcoat not a goddamn thing! I don't romanticize. I write what's real. I tell the kind of stories that don't always get told, especially not from the perspective of a Black man as myself that is navigating the streets, the game, trauma, power, betrayal, and the war for legacy.

What I do ain't just fiction. This shit is survival!

Truth is, being a Black male author in the lit game feels a lot like fighting in the Hunger Games. It's a ruthless battlefield. A war zone, even. The urban fiction industry is dominated by women—female authors, female readers, and female-centered narratives. And while there's respect for that, it leaves cats like myself out in the cold. There ain't many lanes for us. No real support systems. No safety nets. No open arms. Just a sharp pen, raw vision, and a will to out-write and outlast, and to be more prepared.

I'm not here to compete with my lit brothers. (or my lit sisters for that matter) I'm here to build something bigger than me. But the way this industry is set up, they pit us against each other. Like only one of us can make it at a time. Like there's only room for one voice, one pen, one brand. That's a lie. And I'm here to challenge it.

So when you support my books, you're doing more than reading stories. You're breaking a cycle. You're making space for a voice that ain't supposed to exist in this format. Especially not so from the current predicament that I find myself. You're saying: his stories matters, too.

4

This journey ain't easy. But it's necessary. And as long as I got breath and fire in me, I'll keep pushing this pen, writing for the voiceless, the forgotten, the misunderstood, and the feared. And my pen is fire! It's lethal!

Thank you for riding with me.

—Prince (smile)

P.S. To **REALLY** support what I do, buy a book (or books) and buymeacoffee.com/PrinceThaAuthor (smile). I run on caffeine, obsession, anger, pain, emotions, and the will to win at all cost. Once again, thank you for everything!

Montell nearly loses his life all because Roderick and the family's crew had more problems on their hands than they knew, going up against the nigga Khalib and his team. Khalib was the cousin of a street psycho named Kaboni Savage. This was a dude who probably had more bodies under his belt than he had people who liked him. Literally. His family included.

Prologue

THE police eventually made it to the address provided in the 9-1-1 call, Mandy's place. Her dad, J.D, begun to really worry about his daughter and had gotten very restless and on the verge of going into a state of anxiety. There had never been a time Mandy went this long without returning phone calls or text messages, let alone her fathers. He got back in his truck and was en route to Mandy's house again. *I will not return home or do anything until I lay my eyes on my Mandy. I will not!* So thought J.D.

As he pulled onto the road that led through the community, he saw police cars at Mandy's residence while getting closer himself.

"OH NO! NO-NO!" J.D said aloud to himself. *What the hell are the cops doing at my baby's house? I told her about that damn nigger she's dating! Goddamn son of a bitch! Done got my baby into some shit with him! That's why she not picking up. She done let him get her in trouble!* he thought vehemently.

He pulled into the driveway and got out of his car. "Officer, is there a problem here? What's going on?" J.D asked the officer he took notice of to be in charge of the four present.

"Do you live here at this residence, sir?" The officer in charge asked.

"No. But my daughter does. Mandy Barfield. That's her name. I'm John Derby Barfield," he replied and produced identification for the officer. The cop took a look at a piece of paper he'd held after having wrote something on it. Prior to, he'd ran Mandy's license plate number to confirm who lived in the residence. The info J.D. provided matched what he already had.

"Now do you mind telling me what the problem is officer?" J.D. asked.

"Mr. Barfield, the nine-one-one center had gotten a call from an anonymous person claiming to have heard a single gunshot. It was someone claiming to be a 'cable guy', but never specifically provided a name. The caller gave an accurate address—this address—and advised we show up to have a look."

"Well, that's totally far from the truth, because my daughter, is terrified of guns, and have absolutely no reason on God's green earth, to wanna kill herself, let alone, actually do it," responded J.D.

"Well sir, do you know where she might be? And who mentioned *suicide*?" Asked the cop.

"I haven't seen her or spoken to her in a day or so, and you stated *'single gunshot,'* which implies suicide. But wherever she shall be, I'm pretty much more than sure she'll call or contact me and her momma soon," J.D. said.

"Well sir, based on the call, and our repeated attempts to get someone to the door by knocking and ringing the doorbell, we got no replies. And per policy, we will have to break down the door and go inside," the cop informed.

"Y'all fine gentleman go right on ahead and do what you have to. And in the meantime, I'll try to contact her again," responded J.D. then stepped to the side to make more calls to Mandy's number.

The police supervisor gave the nod to the others to proceed with the task at hand. The officers had a hard time but eventually got the door broken open. They combed through the bottom part of the house, then made it up the stairs. This was when the discovery of Mandy's body was made.

The lead officer went back down the stairs and out the front door. "Sergeant Fordham, I need to speak with you sir! Right away!" he requested.

The two stepped to the side and out of ear shot from J.D.

"What you got, Lincoln?" asked the supervisor.

In a whisper he said," Sir, we made a gruesome discovery inside. It's a crime scene. A white female victim sprawled out on the floor upstairs in a pool of blood."

The sergeant was taken aback at the information provided and looked on at his subordinate in shock.

"Hold him here," the supervisor ordered, speaking of J.D. "Let me have a look." The supervisor dashed off heading towards the entrance of the home.

"What the hell is going on? What y'all find?" J.D. demanded to know.

"Sir, I'm sorry. I can't disclose any information outside the order of my supervisor," the subordinate stated and then got quiet as kept.

"Well, when the hell I'm supposed to know what's going on in my own damn daughter's house?" J.D. Spat from frustration. He then stepped back away from the officer and got on his phone to call his wife.

The subordinate who attended to J.D. lowered the volume on his walkie-talkie to prevent J.D. from hearing radio traffic that was subject to come across. The supervisor made the call to central control of a **"187"** with a white female victim who had also appeared to have been sexually assaulted.

J.D. really became impatient and tried to go inside the home, since the supervisor took too long for his comfort to come out. "What in the hell is taking that goddamn officer so long to come back and tell me something?" he demanded to know.

The subordinate never replied. He only stood erect with his left hand palmed over his right and looked on at J.D.

Nearly fifteen minutes later, the crime scene unit and more officers pulled up to the residence. Reluctantly, the supervisor who'd been there from the beginning following the 9-1-1 call, had the duty to tell J.D. the grim news he'd never thought he'd have to hear. He was a devastated man at that point. Forever destroyed beyond all imagination.

One

Chapter 1

Montell made it to Tamron's house and went inside. She knew something was terribly wrong, as his body language showed he was visibly shaken. He knew himself he couldn't mention anything to her about the situation. All he wanted to do with her was to make it known they would stop with the sells of the supply they'd recently gotten from Pete, put the movement on pause for a time being, and lay low. He felt he owed her no reason as to why it was his decision to go this route, and she shouldn't feel the need to ask either. The only thing she had to do was respect the words of her man. But Tamron, would never just settle for Montell simply having it his way without a bitter battle of the sexes.

"Baby what the hell wrong with you? Why you look like that?" Tamron asked.

"It's cool, T-baby, It's cool. Everything good. It is," Montell responded.

"Oh no it's the fuck not! I can clearly see something is not right with you, Montell. Now what's going on?" she pressed.

"Everything cool, Tee. I promise. It's just I had some niggaz step to me trying to put down pressure and extort me. Talking about they want in or else. Them niggaz got me fucked up!" he lied.

"What?! You can't be for real, Montell!" she worded in an angry voice.

"Tee, when you ever known me to play these types of games? I'm being serious," he lied further. "Look Tee, we gonna have to shut everything down for the time being, okay.

We not gonna move or sell anything until I figure out who behind this shit and get me and you a team of straight-shooters to protect us, okay," Montell told Tamron.

Immediately in this instance, the words of Tamron's Uncle Leroy flashed through her mind, *" It's dangerous territory for a female rookie in this line of work, but you know without a doubt, Uncle Leroy right here to help guide you and protect you, just like I gave my brother and you my word I would be. Keep in mind, TeeTee, we only got each other, okay, we only got each other. So with that being said, I want you to always be mindful, you are to get all advice and all else that goes along with it from me, okay. Not your boyfriend, and not from anyone else. Directly from me, okay. Uncle Leroy."*

Tamron couldn't dismiss her uncle's words, even if she wanted to. They were entirely too powerful and held a lot of weight. Once the words of Uncle Leroy took over the words of Montell in her mind," *get all advice and all else that goes along with it from me, not your boyfriend, and not from anyone else, directly from me,* " she gave Montell a once over from head to toe and was in the process of saying something slick to him, but held back for the sake of preventing an argument and further complicating an already bad situation, according to Montell.

Tamron kept in mind to just make a call to Uncle Leroy, and he'd tell her what to do and how to do it. He always had the right answers and proper advice.

"Look, I'll be leaving in a few hours to go home to my mothers house for a day or two. But in the meantime, I'm gonna get with one of my people and have them meet you some place tomorrow or the day after, so they could pick up all the work we got left and put it somewhere else until we get things rolling again, okay," Montell advised.

As he looked at Tamron square in the eyes when he mentioned what the plan was to be, he saw a flash of anger radiate from her eyes then across her face.

"Montell. Have you lost your damn mind! You got me fucked up! I ain't going for no bullshit like that and you know it, nigga! So don't try to play me like that!" Tamron spat.

"Look Tee—"

"—Look Tee, my ass, nigga! I'm not trying to hear that shit, Montell! I'm not! I feel like you trying to pull some bullshit on me now, since you done started to get more money. And how all of a sudden you coming for me with this bullshit right after you met up with that sneaky bitch, NeNe? What's that all about? I need to know," she said.

"Tamron, it ain't the time for us to be arguing with one another. I told you, some niggaz came my way trying to put the press down, and we need to fall back momentarily, until I get some people in place to watch our backs. I ain't got no idea what they know about me or you, and we can't afford to take any chances. Who knows, they may wanna do a home invasion and try to rob something. We got all the work up in here and all that—"

"No we don't!" she cut him off to say.

"What you mean, 'no we don't'?" Montell produced an angry face in retort.

"Just like I said, no we don't. I moved everything a few days ago."

"You did what? Why the fuck you do that?" He seriously demanded an answer.

"Why the fuck *wouldn't* I?" she retorted.

Montell then jumped up from the bed and stood to his feet in Tamron's face. "Tamron!" He called out and grabbed her by both arms. "Why the fuck you do that and I ain't tell you too? HUH!" he shouted.

"So, what, you want me to hold all the dope, take all the risk, and be the fall bitch if the feds was to come! Then, *I'll* be in prison, while you out here doing all you do and being with yo bitches you think I don't know about. Probably NeNe!" She revealed her feelings.

"What! Tamron! You got about two-point-two seconds, to tell me where the fuck you got my damn dope stashed at! Or—"

"—Or what, nigga?" She stood up to him in challenge and said. "What if I don't? Seems to me you got way more problems to be worried about than some damn dope your girlfriend got put away in a safe spot," she said.

"Tamron, stop playing with me, okay! You know I owe Pete all that money."

"And with you or without you, Pete gonna get paid his money. Because my life on the line too. And I can't afford to take no chances with these people," she fired back as the exchange continued.

"Tamron! I'm gonna ask you one more time, okay. Where the fuck is my dope?" Montell demanded very seriously, as if he was about to beat her ass.

They'd fought it out many times in the past. So him spanking on her again was no problem for her. Hell, she felt if he didn't whip her ass every now and then, he didn't love her like he claimed to have, as sassy and sharp-tongued in back talk she was. There had never been a time he put his hands on her when she hadn't forced him to. She always provoked it. As crazy as shit may sound, here is more.

Tamron was a pain-freak, and had mini-orgasms when she forced Montell to slap her around. But the method he preferred to chastise her with was to lash her on the legs and buttocks with a leather belt he kept at her house in the closet. Montell rarely ever hit Tamron in the face, but yes, he had before.

Their verbal confrontation continued. "And what supposed to happen if I don't tell you? Hell it's not like I'm taking it from you. I just got it out of my house and put it in a more low-key area."

Montell looked on at her with daggers in his eyes and ice in his veins behind the drama Tamron brought to him, along with the fact of what was already going on at the very moment with Mandy. Tamron continued to stand up to him in challenge with her head cocked to the right, her hand on her right hip, and her chin pointed upward while looking Montell square in his eyes like, *Now what, nigga!*

As bad as he wanted to, he couldn't hold it any longer. Montell drew back with his hand and fired her ass up! Sparks jumped from her face when he'd smacked her.

Whop!

She went down to the floor and held the right side of her face. Montell was left-handed.

"NIGGA! I know damn well you ain't put your muthafuckin' hands on me, Montell! Oh, hell fuck nawl! HELL FUCK NAWL!!!" she yelled and slammed her hands down hard on her thighs, as she looked up at him angrily.

"Now, stop testing me, Tamron! Where my shit?" he demanded to know.

"MONTELL! Why the fuck you hit me, man! Why the fuck you do that shit! WHY!!!" she yelled again.

"BITCH, DON'T BE QUESTIONIN' ME! I DONE TOLD YOU ALREADY!!! I GOT ENOUGH SHIT TO DEAL WITH RIGHT NOW! AND YOU MADE ME DO IT! YOU ASKED FOR IT! YOU ASKED FOR IT, TAMRON! NOW WHERE THE FUCK YOU PUT MY DOPE AT?" Montell spat vehemently. He yelled to the top of his lungs as he stood over her and pointed his finger in her face.

She continued to sit and hold a look of shock on her face with her mouth agape in total disbelief at it all. It had been a long time to pass since Montell actually put his hands on her in that type of way. The fact was established and she'd gotten the point, he was for real.

Montell raised his hand to smack her again as his intentions was to slap Tamron out until she *un-assed* the whereabouts of his product. The only thing that stopped him from hitting her again was, his cellphone buzzed. It was his worried mother calling him back.

"Yeah momma!" he answered.

"Mar-Mar. What is going on, baby? I really need to know. I really do. Momma is so worried about you. I ain't stopped praying yet. From the time you called until now."

"Ma, I'mma tell you all about it when I get to your house later, okay," he responded.

"Miss Janice, he just hit me. Montell slapped me! He now trying to beat me up some more!" Tamron said, but loud enough for Montell's mother to have heard her.

"MONTELL! You better not hit that girl no more, boy! And I mean it!" Mrs. Janice shouted through the phone at her son.

He mean-mugged Tamron briefly. "Shut the fuck up!" he spat then got back to talking with his mother. "Momma, I'll be down there in a few hours, okay. We can talk then. I got to go now, okay," he lastly said. The call ended.

Tamron continued to look on at him in silence with a serious demeanor. She spoke up," Montell. What has gotten into you, baby? You not yourself. You really not. And it's fucked up because you doing me wrong in the process. It shouldn't be like this. It shouldn't be like this. I don't know what to say or what to do," she said to him.

"All I wanna know is, do you have the dope put away in a safe spot?" he asked.

"Montell, we owe Pete a half million dollars, nigga. My fucking *life* way more valuable than that. You know I got that shit put away in a safe location."

"But why did you move it without asking me first? That was not a smart decision, Tee."

"Because I felt like you was gonna come with some bullshit and try to *X* me out the picture. And not only that. Montell, you don't even respect me as a girlfriend no more. You done got too disrespectful. *Too* disrespectful, man. After I repeatedly told you, I had a major problem with you having NeNe meet up with you and do things for you. And guess what you do? You basically said *fuck me,* and continued to do it anyway. It ain't no doubt in my mind now, I know you two got something going on, or have done something before." She expressed how she felt.

"Tee stop being ridiculous, all right. You know fucking well it's all business."

"All business huh?"

"All business."

"So why the fuck, I got to continue to hear about a rumor being spread, that the bitch going 'round bragging to all the other girls about how she sucked your dick in your truck while y'all was on the way back from Six Flags one Saturday, the Saturday that I can't seem to forget, when you never answered your damn phone! How you explain that?" she fired back. "You know the bitch couldn't wait to rub some shit like this in my muthafuckin' face. And not only that she don't even seem to try to call me or nothing anymore. I assume she just go to you now for everything. Now ain't that a bitch! My own home-girl, got *complete* access to all she wants with *my* man!" she added while still seated on the floor, mostly out of fear he would smack her ass again.

"Like I said, ain't shit going on with me and NeNe." he defended.

"Okay, whatever Montell. Just go on ahead and do what you need to do and work out the situation you dealing with now. I'll be here. And everything safe. Don't worry about anything. I'll call you later today and we can talk then. What you need me to do in the meantime?" Tamron asked him.

"Just stop all movement for right now, keep everything put away, and check in with me if any of your people got some serious money they wanna spend, like for a whole unit or better, okay."

Tamron continued to sit on the floor and shake her head from left-to-right in disgust at the thought of the situation her relationship with Montell had turned out to become. She truly couldn't believe it. She knew he was lying to her about his problem he faced, and of the rumor behind him and her friend. But she couldn't prove anything. At least not at the time.

She had a solution, a bona fide plan on how she would get even with Montell for hitting her yet again, and for cheating on her with one of her best friends, then, get ahead in her game plan on how she would continue on about handling business.

Although the situation was bad for Montell, things was good for Tamron. She felt it in her spirit that it was.

Chapter 2

Roderick was back in Atlanta and out of harms way from the battlefield of Philly. At least for the time being. He and Jamie met up at Seduction City before the doors were to open for business this day. They had a conversation about many things. It mostly surrounded their lives at the time.

Geno and Razor was also at the lounge themselves and in the office with Roderick and Jamie. To prevent them from hearing anything the two close friends wanted to discuss amongst themselves, they stepped out and paced around the parking lot to talk.

"Yo Jamie, that bitch-ass nigga, Rico, finally got it boy," Roderick brought up.

"What!" he expressed excitement. "Say it ain't so, nigga." Jamie wanted more.

"Yeah man. Word is, they hit that pussy thirty-two times with sharp steel."

"I wonder who got to him? Could it had been J-Smack people?"

"Nah. It wasn't them. It was the nigga's own people that got him."

"His own people got him? What you mean by that Rod?" Jamie asked with a slight chuckle.

"His own people. The nigga joined a gang while up in there."

"What! He was too pussy to stand on his own two?"

"Hell, you know if he was too pussy to do his own *time* without ratting on us, what make you think he wasn't too *pussy* to do a bid on his own?"

"How you find out about all this?"

"So, you don't know nothing about any of this shit?" He asked a question with a question.

"Nope."

"Damn bro. I got to catch you up on everything," Roderick stated, and went into the details of two situations he'd been all too familiar with.

"So look. Me, my sister Lea, and a couple of our other guys, had went out to Atlantic City to enjoy the night one Saturday. But while we was on the way, Lea gets a call from one of our people locked in the feds, our cousin Josh. He and I ain't had a chance to chop it up in a couple of years. We got him on speaker, catching up on a few things. I asked him where they got him at now? He told me they had him out in Cali, at the Victorville spot. For some reason the name rang a bell in my head, and I was busy trying to remember what was so special about the name, *'Victorville.'* I told Josh to give us a minute or two and to call us back or we'd call him one. I pull out my line then hit Montell, because I know the nigga got an outstanding memory on shit like that. As soon as I mentioned *'Victorville' Cali'* to him, he immediately let me know what the name be all about. The name came up in a conversation the three of us had one day at Montell place, the time when he looked up Rico on the BOP website."

"Damn sho' did, Rod! It damn sho' did!"

"So, once Mo let me know what the particular name related to, I hit my people back from my line—he got a jack himself in there—and asked him do he know a nigga named Rico? Cuz didn't know him by *that* name per se. But once I described him, he then knew who I as talking about. They don't call the nigga by 'Rico' no more. He went by his 'Crip name'—*'Blue Dot'*—as he'd gotten down since getting off PC," Roderick said.

"Ain't that a bitch! Them white folks used him to knock off two enterprises, and then, them wack-ass gang niggaz, just embrace him with open arms," Jamie remarked after learning of Rico's history of gang banging.

"Man, what you talking about," commented Roderick, in agreement with Jamie.

Rod continued. "Anyway, my cousin say that the bitch-ass nigga had big-boy rank in that Crip shit. Say the nigga was an 'OG,' Jamie!"

"You got to be lying, Rod!"

"No hell I ain't! I bullshit you not, my nigga! Real Talk. Rico was well respected on the blue team," Roderick stated.

"So how did word get out that he ratted?"

"You already know I had to get my hands in on it somewhere. I requested court certified documents from our case. Then, I had them mailed directly to Josh from the court. He got with the veteran OG niggaz over the Crips there, and they confirmed, true indeed— 'Blue Dot'—ate that cheese! He was put on a plate from there. They eventually got him. Poked that bitch thirty-two times, son!" Roderick smiled as he told story again. He delighted in telling the story so much, that he felt the need to be redundant with it.

Jamie smiled from ear-to-ear himself. He commented," That's good for that snitch-bitch! He got everything he deserved."

Roderick continued on about the other story he'd went through while in AC. "Hey Jamie. That ain't it though, my nigga. I got another story to tell you."

"Oh, you do? Damn boy! You can begun a career as a writer with all these fire-ass stories you got, my nigga. What now?"

"Yeah, while in AC, and leaving out the door of a resort that hosted some boxing matches, me and Lea on the way to gamble in the casino part. This shit was too much of a coincidence here. Guess who I bump into?"

"Who that bruh?"

"That sucker-ass nigga, Eric!"

"Now boy I know you got to be bullshitting me!" remarked Jamie. "For real! You got to be!"

"Yo, I bullshit you not. He had some Spanish looking female with him,"

"What happen to the Warden bitch he stole from Montell?" Jamie asked.

"I couldn't tell you about that. All I know is what I saw," Roderick let out.

"And you ain't say shit to him?" Jamie asked.

Roderick sucked his teeth then remarked," My nigga, you know I had to say something to the pussy! Me and him got to hitting! Nigga took off on me first, Jamie," informed Roderick, and cut through the chase on all that happened.

"That arrogant bastard ain't never been scared to throw his hands," commented Jamie.

"We all got locked up in the parking lot after the police sprayed our asses with that mace shit. Burnt my got-damn eyes Jamie," Roderick made known.

"Ha ha ha ha! I know that shit did boy. I know it did. So the Spanish bitch got locked up too?"

"The Spanish bitch got locked up too," Roderick fast responded. "But here is the thing. I had Montell on video Chat the whole time, from the moment I noticed it was Eric. Mo cursed the nigga out. I also had Lea take a picture of Eric's tag number, so I can have someone look up his address. We definitely got to cross paths again. Our court date next month," mentioned Roderick.

"Shit Rod. We probably got a chance to touch the fuck-nigga now, long before then, homey. Along with what he did to Mo, he fucked us over too. All that muthafuckin' money we'd made and he just run off with it like that. The pussy left all of us with our dicks in the dirt!"

"Hell yeah. Hell yeah he did. He got to pay. This shit personal to me bruh. Real talk," spat Jamie.

"Me too bro. That's why I got on the nigga's ass the way I did. But I wanna really do the nigga dirty. Matter of fact, I AM gonna do him dirty! That bitch-ass nigga done fucked up big time!"

"You got hitter's on speed dial up in Philly?" asked Jamie.

"Every since that shit happen to my brother and our cousin, it put me in a different space, in a position of power. I got to put somebody on top of the mission."

"Just do what you got to do, Rod. You'll be doing the team a favor. We down to three now from five. I like to call us 'Three The Hard Way'," Jamie let out and then smiled behind his own words.

The two continued to talk and plan ahead for how they wanted things to go with Seduction City. Any unnecessary squabbles with the cops or otherwise was not something needed. They had to continue and avoid confrontations at all cost.

Chapter 3

End All Be All...

Mandy had been brutally murdered in her own home. Her family and colleagues alike mourned her death. The stab wounds she'd sustained from the assailant's knife, was enough to make a everyone cry that knew her. She was DOA! The lead homicide detective, Brian Lynn Saxton, launched an intense investigation, along with evidence gathering which took place. The fact was overwhelmingly clear, she'd been brutally raped prior to being brutally murdered. And the guilty person had no other intent other than what he'd done.

There was nothing taken from the residence, and the only possible motive the police could think of was, either they had a serial rapist/killer on the loose, or some scorned boyfriend had flipped and lost it in the heat of the moment. Either way, Detective Saxton, was determine," with might and main," to crack the case, make an arrest, and get a conviction to such senseless and horrendous crime. Those was his words to J.D. Barfield, Mandy's father. He went to the home of the victim's parents a day later.

"Throughout the thorough search of the house, there was five kilos of narcotics that had been discovered, $85,000 in cash, mostly small bills, and two firearms—handguns," the detective reported.

J.D. damn near went berserk over the fact, once he'd been made aware of illegal contraband being found in his murdered daughter's home.

How could Mandy be so foolish and get herself caught up with that damn black-ass monkey of a boyfriend she dated! That damn nigger done killed my baby and forgot his shit behind as he ran like the coward he is after doing so! Leaving his damn drugs and guns in her house, J.D. thought to himself as the detective related the articles of evidence found at the crime scene.

"Mister. Barfield, do you know of any boyfriend your daughter may have had?" ask detective Saxton.

"Yeah, I do. That's who all the illegal stuff belongs to. My daughter ain't have nothing to do with no drugs, sir. Mandy worked at the bank," J.D. responded in his deep southern accent.

"I'm aware of her place of employment sir. The boyfriend you mentioned. Who is he?" Mr. Saxton ask again.

"I don't really know his whole name. Only met him once. Montell is the first name. My wife there," J.D. pointed at Carol as she stood at a distance in the front yard of the house while the two men talked," she knows more about the relationship than I do. All I know is, he's a black guy named Montell. They met in college some years back. And as I said, I met him once," J.D. Reiterated. "Come here Carol," J.D. called out to this wife. "This fine policeman here wants to know about the boyfriend of Mandy. The *black* guy," J.D. stated.

"Hello ma'am. How are you? I'm sorry for your loss. I'm detective, Saxton, and the one in charge of investigating this case," he begun.

"Nice to meet your Mister. Saxton," Mrs. Barfield stated in a low tone of voice.

"Mandy's boyfriend. Do you have any information you could provide me about him?" he asked.

J.D. butted in before she could answer. "Tell her what y'all found in Mandy's house Mister. Saxton," he uttered and motioned with his finger from the detective to his wife as if to say, *go on and tell her, let her know.*

"Ma'am there was a large quantity of illegal drugs found in the house along with a large amount of cash, and a few handguns," related Mr. Saxton.

"SAY WHAT! MY LORD! This is too much on me," Mrs. Carol admitted and then was brought to tears behind the revelations. J.D. had to grab hold of his wife to prevent her from collapsing to the ground in grief.

It took Mrs. Barfield a few minutes to gather herself before she could continue with speaking to the detective. She managed to get it together long enough to provide a few reports.

"Yes, Mandy's boyfriend. He is a black guy, as mentioned," Carol reluctantly stated in J.D's presence," and they'd dated for years off and on—"

"For years probably more *off* than *on*, sir," J.D. butted in once more.

"But for the most part, they were happy with one another. I assume," Mrs. Barfield concluded on the details of the relationship. "His name is Montell, Montell McNeal," Mrs. Carol informed.

Mr. Saxton begun taking notes. "You say 'Montell McNeal', right?" asked Mr. Saxton for confirmation.

"Yes, that's correct" replied Carol.

"And how am I spelling 'McNeal'—'N-e-a-l' or N-e-i-l'?" he asked.

"That'll be 'N-e-a-l,' sir," Mrs. Carol spelled it out for him as he continued to take down notes.

J.D. looked on at his wife with a stern face and burning with anger on the inside, being Carol knew far more about Mandy's boyfriend and their relationship than she'd let off. He hated how Carol condoned the interracial love affair, as opposed to condemning it "for what it was," as he always had.

Mrs. Carol had felt the angry energy that radiated from her husband's demeanor and body language. She simply kept her head low and continued to answer the questions

Detective Saxton had for they regarding the murder of their dear Mandy.

Mr. Saxton lifted his head and looked they in the eyes back and forth, as he had another revelation to let out. "Are you two aware that the victim, Mandy, was pregnant as well?" he asked.

"What!" J.D. and Mrs. Carol responded at the same time. She burst into tears again as their entire world had seemingly came crushing down on them.

"That would've been our very first grandchild," Mrs. Carol stated. J.D. didn't utter one word on it. He only kept quiet.

Mr. Saxton continued," Yes, the autopsy revealed that indeed, she was pregnant with a child."

"Well damn. She'd already suffered major stab wounds, and now you telling us she had to be butchered more, an autopsy for crying out loud," stated J.D.

"Mister Barfield, it's Federal law, all homicides require an autopsy performed on the victims," informed Mr. Saxton. J.D. had no response to those facts. He only hated the reality that his sweet Mandy became a homicide statistic and no longer alive to be with them. It's absolutely a hurtful thing for a parent to be the ones who have the duty to bury their child.

Mr. Saxton went on with his line of questions for the Barfields for about fifteen minutes more and did the best he could to console and bring a sense of ease to them in their time of mourning. The investigative crew Mr. Saxton lead, had collected plenty of evidence at the Crime Scene. They had blood samples, Mandy's cellphone, sneaker footprints, fingerprints, and a plethora of other material to run DNA testing on or other forensics so to narrow down exactly who the killer could possibly be.

Chapter 4

Montell's criminal record had been investigated, and Mandy's coworkers was thoroughly questioned as well. The next move the police was to make was to locate the whereabouts of Montell for questioning, to see what all he may have to say. But he was four hours away laying low at his mothers home in Albany, Georgia, and unavailable for any and everybody, except for Tamron and his mother.

The day before, upon making it to his mothers house, he let her know everything he'd walked into at Mandy's home and all he'd done at the point of finding her in such way. He left out the part about the drugs and the guns he'd stashed there and subsequently forgot to grab upon exiting the house.

Montell was in a mess and truly didn't know what to do. He felt strongly there was nothing he could do to prevent them from pinning his pregnant girlfriend's murder on him, and the prosecutor, would absolutely seek the death penalty without a doubt. He was doomed, and he knew it.

Montell's mother, suggested he go ahead and turn himself in to the police, or at least go talk to them before they list him as a suspect and issue a warrant. She thought along the notion," *if you ain't did nothing wrong, then you have nothing to worry about.*" That was what she thought and prayed to God for him to do.

"Momma, that won't be happening," he murmured somberly.

"Why not?" she replied.

"Because it's a few things I haven't told you yet. I left them out so we could talk about them and figure out a way to help me come from under this mess once they bring the hammer down on me."

She paused extensively before speaking out again. "Montell, I know damn well you ain't lied to me about something, son," she blurted out.

"No-no-no, momma. Why would I do that? I would never lie to you about something like this momma."

"So, what's the problem then?" Mrs. Janice demanded to know.

"Momma, I had been staying at Mandy's house on the regular, so, I know the police got my fingerprints, my clothes I had over there, probably a sample or two of my DNA from inside her body, my phone number and the text messages we'd exchanged and all other material that connected us—"

"But if you didn't do it or had nothing to do with it, why be concerned about any of that?" she cut him off to ask.

"Because momma, I'm so terrified they may gun me down once they come to arrest me, or frame me in the courts and sentence me to death! That's why I'm concerned. This *is* Georgia!" Montell revealed his fears.

"That may seem to be a reality at the present time. But don't you ever, and I mean don't you ever, deny the power of the Lord. EVER!" Mrs. Janice shouted the last word. She'd been hit with the Holy Spirit right there in the moment.

Montell begun to cry. His mother grabbed him by both hands, squeezed them tightly and begun to pray. She recited the Lord's Prayer and the 23rd Psalms. Once the praying was complete, she urged Montell, to tell her through the spirit of God, all he'd not spoken on already. He reluctantly begun.

"Momma, I'm sorry to have to tell you this, but I had started dealing drugs," he revealed.

His mother got silent as ever, then briefly spoke out again. "So, your life was in danger and some people came for you to kill you, but couldn't get you and took your girlfriend's life instead?" she asked.

"No momma. I wish it was a situation simple to explain like that. I'd been went to the police by now. But that's not what happened," Montell said, ignorant of all his mother was getting at.

"So, what actually did you *not* tell me, son?" Mrs. Janice asked her son in a way for him to give her a straight answer.

"Momma, I had some drugs, money, and guns stashed at her house," he finally revealed.

"Son, no you didn't. How this happened?" she wanted him to explain more. "None of that belonged to you, okay."

"It just happened that way momma. I felt the need to keep everything in a safe spot, and at the time, her house was the safest location," he said.

"Son, I thought you and Tamron was together?"

"And we are. But I had something going on with the white girl too. The thought never crossed my mind that she would be killed one day, and the police run a search on her house and stumble up on drugs, money and guns."

"So in other words, if they don't get you on one thing, they would on another?" his mother asked bluntly.

"That's exactly what I fear the most, momma. I know without doubt, that my black-ass, is going back to prison," Montell expressed somberly.

His mother paused and didn't respond to his words, as she didn't know what to tell him. She dropped her head low and shook it from side to side as she and her son sat and talked on the couch in her living room. Mrs. Janice spoke out again.

"Well son, truth be told to you, it's not a good idea to be here for too much longer, because you know they will be coming looking for you at some point soon, and especially so behind a white girl getting killed. Your momma and your step-daddy definitely do not need any unnecessary attention from the man. And you already know, if they try to pin those drugs and guns on you, was it only one gun you say or more than one?" his mother switched positions from saying what she felt would occur to asking a question.

"I had two pieces of protection in Mandy's house, ma," Montell responded to his mother.

"*Dog-gonnet*, son! You got yourself in a mess, baby. A mess, you hear me! But no matter what, momma here all right. Momma-is-here," Mrs. Janice assured him in an uplifting tone to encourage her son to keep a positive spirit.

"MAN!" Montell blurted out in frustration. It was something he'd forgotten, an important part to his reality and freedom.

"What son? What now?" Mrs. Janice asked.

"I still got almost two years of probation left. I'm gonna definitely be violated. I may as well go right on ahead and begin preparing myself to go back to prison. I didn't know until the last minute what all my sentence was," he confirmed grimly. "I'mma be sure to get everything in order and be situated before I turn myself in though," he'd added.

"Son, why you thinking on a negative level? Everything may work out in your favor. Just trust and believe. Let God do all the driving for you, okay," his mother said. "But baby, in the meantime, why won't you get in touch with your cousin them in Delaware and be on your way up there? You gone need time to get it together in the event they try to come pick you up for questioning or for whatever reason they may have. No matter what son, we don't claim negativity, and your momma gonna continue to pray and ask the good Lord to deliver you from any potential trouble which looms over your head," Mrs. Janice said.

"I know that's right, Momma," Montell agreed with his mother to appease her in a sense, being they differed greatly in terms of faith and religion.

But no matter what, he had always held the utmost respect for the belief and views of his mother, the good Christian and God-fearing woman that she was.

Montell gave his mother about $50,000 in cash to hold and $35,000 in silver ingots to hold as well. He kept $20,000 for himself in cash to travel with. Mandy had roughly $175,000 in the bank that belonged to him, and another $30,000 in CD's. He knew it was $205,000 to the wind, as he'd never see any of it again. The personal money, he had not a concern for, but the $500,000 that was owed to Pete, was the only issue which rested on his mind. As long as Tamron kept the remaining thirty-five kilos of Meth, the five kilos of Molly, and those pills in a safe spot, then he felt, all would be ok.

She needed to do all he told her as well, and not bring any additional problems his way as the situation play out. But there was no telling how Tamron is to act, once the facts of his ordeal come out.

Knowing her, she'd find more issues in the fact that Montell was strongly involved with a white girl over her. That's how shallow her thinking was at times. But now, she's in the circle of heavy drug suppliers and had a police uncle on her side to protect her and to also carry out the plans which he had in mind which additionally included his niece, she was somewhat subject to do a different dance to the tune being played. Only time would tell.

Chapter 5

One Week Later...

"This is channel Five news with an update on the brutal rape and murder of a thirty-five year-old promising female whose life was taken in her own home on Lake Lanier Lane roughly one week ago to the day...

—Initially, the police had no suspects nor any leads to implicate a possible suspect to be charged for these horrendous acts, but upon the launch of an investigation and a thorough search of the victim, Mandy Jane Barfield's, house, authorities were able to gather an overwhelming amount of direct evidence, sufficient to be issued a warrant for questioning of a possible suspect. Police has put out a warrant for this man, Montell Jermaine McNeal, the assumed boyfriend of the victim, as the two had an on again off again love affair, dating back to their days in college, according to the parents of the victim, John Derby Barfield and Carol Monroe Barfield...

—The victim had a prominent position at First Trust Bank downtown Atlanta, as a Manager. Records show the person wanted for questioning in this case, the African-American boyfriend, had served time in Federal and state prisons for an array of white collar/criminal schemes he and a host of his criminal associates was convicted of...

—In addition to the killing, the police discovered a large quantity of illegal drugs, two firearms, and an abundance of cash inside Miss. Barfield's home. The police had initially suspected there possibly was a home invasion with robbery

as the potential motive, but ruled it out upon being made aware by the medical examiner, indeed, the victim was sexually assaulted, and nothing had been taken from the home. If you have any information about this crime, or of the whereabouts of Montell Jermaine McNeal, please contact the authorities. This is Casey Furlough reporting for the Channel Five News Team:"

***

GENO WAS THE first to speak out on what he heard on the news.

"What the fuck!" Exclaimed Geno. "I know damn well, that that nigga Montell, ain't fucked around, and got himself caught up in no shit like this!" Geno yelled out for everybody around to hear him. "Razor! You see this shit right there? No wonder the nigga ain't been seen or heard from in the last week or so. He got problems on his hands to deal with. Wait to that nigga Jamie get here and find out about this shit with his dude. Montell's ass on the way back to prison. He might get the fucking death penalty over some shit like this!" Geno let out to his close friend and personal bodyguard, Razor.

The two was the first to get to the club for the day and turned on the TV in the office to watch the news. Roderick had gone back to Philly to square away a few things there, as he normally traveled back and forth at least three to four times monthly.

Geno maintained a heavy presence at Seduction City, as he loved the fact of being in ownership now and having exclusive access to some of the baddest strippers ATL had to offer. Another thing Geno had going good for him none of the others didn't. He was without a main girlfriend in his life, so there was no obligation he owed to a relationship, and he enjoyed the luxury of being without drama either.

On this particular day, it was the first time the police had named Montell as a suspect and listed him wanted for

35

questioning. He took the advice of his mother and went up north to the state of Delaware to hide out from the police. He and Tamron keep contact by phone, as he had her under the impression he was still down in Albany, at his mom's house and not a thousand plus miles up the east coast in the capital city of Dover of the state.

Montell was slick about how he done things in a lot of ways. He and NeNe, kept in contact as well, as he'd caused her to become dependent upon him for many reasons such as how she was able to stay supplied and keep a steady flow of income. The day he had NeNe to meet Tamron so she could pick up those two bricks of meth, he sold one whole, and let her keep the other to break down into ounces and be sold in this way, so NeNe could earn more profit. The rumors of the two was in fact true, but Tamron had never caught them together on no level, so, she had no right to accuse.

***

WORD GOT AROUND pretty quickly, Montell was on the news and the police wanted to question him. Geno damn sure let Jamie know the very moment he stepped in the door.

"Yeah Jamie, I don't know if you seen it or not, but man, Montell done fucked up and got his ass in deep trouble with the law."

"Huh! What's going on?" questioned Jamie.

"*Our* business partner, was just on the news," Geno revealed mockingly.

"Say what! On the news? Trouble with the law? About what?" Jamie responded.

"They say the police wanna question him about some white chick being killed and dope being found in her house."

"Man! You got to be bullshitting, Geno!" Jamie muttered in a shocking type way.

"No, the fuck I ain't. Why would you say some shit like that on a nigga's name, shawdy! You know I don't get down like," Geno responded.

"Let me hit this nigga and see what's up," Jamie said, and pulled his phone from his waistline and dialed the contact number to Montell's line. It had been changed or disconnected. Jamie looked on at the screen of his phone as if something was wrong on his end. He tried a second time. Same results. *What the fuck!* he thought. *Mo done changed his number and ain't say shit to us about it. Let me try Rod and see if he been in touch with him lately. It's been about a week and we ain't seen or heard shit from this nigga since,* he further thought.

Roderick answered his phone," Yeah what's up J?"

"Aye, say Rod, you ain't heard from Mo lately, have you?" Jamie had asked.

"Nah, I ain't. Come to think about it, it's been about a week or two since I last seen or heard from that nigga. Why? What's up?" Roderick wanted to know.

"Because I just tried to call him and his number ain't no good anymore. Plus, I just got to the club and Geno told me some shit that really fucked me up, bruh," Jamie mentioned.

"Word. Really fucked you up like what?" Roderick had asked.

"Geno say, he was watching the news, and Montell's picture popped up on the screen. Say the police got a warrant out for him for questioning about some white girl being raped and killed—"

"Get the fuck outta here!" Roderick shouted out and cut Jamie off just before he completed his words.

"Yeah man. That's what I've been told by Geno, he and Razor," Jamie commented.

"Jamie, it wasn't the white girl Mandy he was fucking with, was it?" Roderick asked.

"You know what, I don't even know right off. Wait. Let me ask Geno," Jamie propositioned, putting Roderick on hold briefly.

"Say Geno. By chance, you didn't happen to remember what was the name of the white girl who was killed do you?" he asked.

Geno looked at Razor as they tried to remember. Then, it hit Geno," Yeah, I remember something about the last name being, Barfield, I believe," Geno responded.

Jamie went back to talking to Roderick. "Yeah Rod, Geno said something about a last name being 'Barfield'," Jamie relayed.

"Damn Jamie. That's Mandy's last name," Roderick stated

"I'm trying to remember who she is?" Jamie said.

"You remember the white chick who came by his place the time we was there and she brought us that pizza and those wings, don't you?" Roderick asked.

"Oh yeah, I remember it being a white girl, but I ain't never know her name," responded Jamie.

"Well, that was Mandy, the white girl he'd been fucking with since college," Roderick had said.

"I wonder how the fuck Montell get caught up in some shit like this?" Jamie stated.

"Your guess is just as good as mine, bro. Your guess just as good as mine," Roderick spoke up to say.

"I'mma go on the internet and see what all the shit talking about, then I'll hit you back, and we can try to get in touch with Montell together," Jamie stated.

"I'm with you on it bro. Just hit me back, and in the meantime, I'll try him through Messenger or his email accounts. That nigga got to tell us something, J."

"I know that's right. That nigga got to tell us something," Jamie repeated the words of his friend and they ended the call.

"So, what Rod say on that?" Geno asked.

"He don't really know anything, but he helped me remember who Mandy was. I'm about to go online now and see what the news is on the situation," he came back with in reply, searching Google to know the full story.

He looked at the brief news clip that Channel 5 News had broadcast. Jamie looked on in absolute shock at the facts surrounding the situation. Not only did the issue of the rape and murder cause him to became gravely concerned for Montell, but the issue of the drugs and the guns made him really worry too. Damn Montell. He uttered to himself. Boy you done really fucked up my nigga. Really fucked up. He had added and shook his head from side to side.

Jamie didn't really know what to make of the situation. But if anything, he did know Montell would eventually get in contact with him and let his side of the story be heard. Jamie maintained a sense of belief in his friend, to know Montell didn't have no reason to rape someone, let alone, kill them. And especially not someone he was involved with. A fucking white girl, in Georgia! No-No. Ain't no motherfucking way!

THE DIRTY SIDE OF MONEY 3 | PRINCE

Chapter 6

On The Other Side Of The City...

TAMRON got a call from Kay-Kay. She was eager to be the first one to report to Tamron on what the situation was with Montell. "What's up bitch," Tamron answered.

"Tamron. You been watching the news today?" Kay-Kay asked.

"No. Why? Should I have?" Tamron replied.

"Bitch hell yeah you should have!" Kay-Kay responded.

Tamron spring up from her laying position on the bed to now sitting and engaged in the video chat with Kay-Kay and looking on at her facial features as she talked. "What the world going on, Kay?" she urged her friend to stop beating around the bush and tell her what the fuck was up.

"Bitch. How about, '*Twelve,*' got a warrant out on your dude, behind some white girl being raped and killed!" Kay-Kay related.

"Say what! Kay—"

"Tamron, now you know I don't play when it come to some Shit like this, girl. I don't play," Kay-Kay cut Tamron's words short to say right on cue, as if she knew what her friend was about to say next.

"Let me call you back in a minute, okay," Tamron stated and ended the call before Kay-Kay was able to say another word.

Tamron then called the one person she knew who would be able to give her accurate and detailed facts, especially about a crime, before she was to call Montell and say something to him about it and not be told all the truth. It was a call to be made to her police uncle, Leroy.

"Hello Tee. How you doing?" he answered?

"Hey Uncle Leroy. I called because I'm trying to find out something," she said.

"I had something I wanted to ask you any how. You called at a good time."

"Oh I did?" she replied to the remark of her uncle.

"Yep. I wanted to ask about that boyfriend of yours. You say his name was, Montell, right?" he asked of his niece.

"Yeah. Montell is his name," she responded.

"And you say, he been to the Feds about some white-collar stuff he and his friends had going on, right?" The uncle asked again.

"Yes sir. That be the truth."

"He wouldn't happen to be a 'Montell-Jermaine-McNeal' we now looking for, would he?' Uncle Leroy asked a third question.

"Yes Uncle Leroy. That's his full name," Tamron confirmed somberly. "That's why I called you, to find out a thing or two. I got a call from one of my girlfriends and she, told me Montell, was on the news and wanted in connection about a rape and murder," Tamron said.

"That's *exactly* the truth," Leroy stated. "I'm about five minutes away from you now, TeeTee. We'll talk when I get there, ok. Although I'm old-school, you know I'm 'Kevin Gates' with mine, baby girl. I don't talk on phones! I'll see you in a few, okay," he lastly said and disconnected the call.

Tamron couldn't hold it any longer. She burst into tears and immediately dialed Montell's number she had to reach him at, one not the original. *I knew it had to be more to that shit than he lied to me about. All the motherfucka had to do was tell me the truth, that's it. I'm already down with him no matter what. But for some reason, Montell don't get the picture, and think I'm not.* Tamron related as she talked to herself in waiting for Montell to pick up in answering the phone. He finally accepted her call on video chat.

"What's up, Tee," Montell greeted with a look about his face which showed he was very exhausted and stressed out behind the grim reality he now faced. Tamron didn't say anything and had only stared into the phone looking on at him and had no control of the tears which poured down her face now.

He had music playing in the background of the room he was in. It was a song by rapper J. Cole, *Middle Child.*

"What's up, Tee? Huh," he let out then allowed a side of his emotions to show with a tear rolling down from his left eye.

Tamron spoke up. "Montell, please tell me what in the hell going on?" she asked of him.

He shrugged his shoulders and continued to keep quiet, as he knew she would speak on all she had to say of what she'd found out.

"I got Kay-Kay and other people calling me talking about, they seen you on the news and shit. And the police got a warrant on you for questioning about a fuckin' 'rape' and 'murder' of a fuckin' white girl!" Tamron mentioned and paused long enough for Montell to say something.

He continued to keep quiet and only looked on at her as they both glared into the lens of the camera. He finally said something, but nothing related to what he was being questioned about.

"Hey, you still got everything put away in a safe spot, right?" he asked.

She continued to pause then responded," Yeah. I do. But I asked you a question, Montell. Ain't you gonna answer that for me?" she asked.

"Look Tee, I haven't done nothing wrong, ok. I ain't done nothing wrong. I promise to tell you all about it in due time. Just please be patient with me on this, ok. It's not bad as it may seem because I ain't done nothing wrong. Just keep that in mind sweetie," he responded.

"Well if you ain't done nothing wrong and don't got nothing to worry about, then, why you running? And why you don't wanna tell me what the problem is? And who is this white girl? You know her or something?" Tamron asked.

"Tamron, please baby. Now is not the time, ok. I'll be back in Atlanta in a few days and we can talk about everything then. But for now, I really just need to think and rest. That's all. Think and rest," Montell responded.

"So, I guess you not down in Albany any longer either, huh?"

He kept silent and didn't say a word, just continued to stare.

Tamron's uncle pulled up and was parked in the back of the house like he always had done. He got out and made his way to the back door.

"You know what, we can just talk later like you said. I'll call you back, okay," she declared and ended the call to go let her Uncle Leroy into the house. She knew he wouldn't want her having anyone know of the type of conversations the two was now in the habit of having.

"Hey Uncle Leroy. How you doing?" she greeted.

"I'm fine, TeeTee. I'm mighty fine. I thank you for having me over on such short notice. As you know it's business," the uncle stated. "So, look, that boyfriend, he's in some deep shit, TeeTee," Leroy begun, as he propped himself up on the counter top with his arm stretched out fully and the other on his hip.

"What exactly is going on with him, Uncle Leroy?" Tamron wanted a straight answer.

"He's in a fucked-up predicament. But at this particular point, he's only wanted for questioning. I know for a fact once he's in custody, things will certainly change. The victim in the case, a white female named, Mandy Barfield, she was raped and then stabbed in the chest and gut ten or more times. On top of that she was pregnant too," the uncle had said.

"Say what! Somebody actually raped her, and then stabbed the girl to death, even though she was pregnant! What kind of person would do something sick like that anyway? Never mind the pregnant part!" Tamron blurted.

"A damn monster! A goddamn monster! And we treating it as such too, like we are trying to track down a motherfucking monster. US at APD. The Hall County Sheriff's Department. And The GBI, TeeTee," responded the uncle. Tamron shook her head slowly from side to side behind the words of her uncle.

He continued," Now Teetee, this boyfriend of yours, tell Uncle Leroy exactly, when was the last time you talked to him?" he questioned.

"Honestly Uncle Leroy, it was about a week ago when he came by here one morning and was acting very strange. I asked him what the problem was, and he'd told me a lie about some other big-time guys, had sent some people to see him, to threaten and try to press him in extortion for money. But something just didn't seem true about it to me. Montell was too paranoid for that type of issue to have occurred. I felt it was more to it because he called his mother, and if it was some street beef, why would he do that? He never did something like it in the past. And then he goes on trying to get me to hand over to him all of the supply we got left. Like I was about to let his ass leave me hanging out here with nothing. It's a good thing I took the advice you gave me and relocated everything."

"That's a good thing, Tee. That's a very good thing. I'm glad you listened. I told you, Uncle Leroy wouldn't never lead you in the wrong direction. But anyway, you didn't tell him where you got the stuff put up at, did you?"

"No. I didn't. He tried to press me to tell him, but I didn't," Tamron said, but left out the part to her uncle about

Montell beating on her the way he had. She knew her police uncle wouldn't have taken it too well.

"Tee, listen to me, okay, and listen to me well. I want you to kill any and all forms of communication with that guy, okay. That is to happen immediately! No phone conversation, no social media, no nothing, okay. It won't be good for business for us moving forward. The closer he is to you, the more exposure it will be on me and all you and I got going on," he declared, then gestured with his finger back and forth between he and Tamron.

"You don't need no negative attention period. That guy is in a world of trouble, Tee. A world of trouble! We don't need no links between him and you, because that puts me in the mix. Do I make myself clear on that Tee?" Leroy asked as he looked on at his niece with a straight look about his face.

"Yes, Uncle Leroy. We clear on that," Tamron had replied.

"Now, the part about the business. You still loaded, right?"

"Yes."

"And the connect you told me about. How well do they know you?" the uncle wanted to know.

"I won't say that he knows me pretty well, but I can say he trusts me to do the right thing, as far as business in concerned. And he trust me to keep Montell on track," Tamron responded.

"That part right there. The connect. Do they know anything about your boyfriend's new troubles he now in?" Leroy questioned.

"I wouldn't think so, because then, he'll cut his ass off and wont deal with us any longer," she expressed in a concerned way.

"Of course, it's not a question rather the head guy would cut all contact between he and Montell, the boyfriend of yours. Hell, he'd probably have his ass killed in the process, once his money is paid to him. A half million you two owe, right?"

"Yes. A half million is the tab owed, and it seems like the duty gonna be on me to pay it. I've got to be the one to get rid of all that shit we got left," Tamron stated.

"TeeTee, the duty is on you now to get rid of everything and see to it the main man gets his money. I suggest you get in touch with him soon too, and let him know all that is going on, and that your boyfriend is no longer available. *You* are from here on out. Be straight with the connection. Tell him *everything*, except the parts about me. Better yet, set up a meeting between you and him, so the two of you could talk, face to face, and he'll be able to see you for who you truly are, outside the presence of your boyfriend."

"But Uncle Leroy, the head man, Pete, he's way down in Colombia. We've only met the people he got in place here in the states," Tamron responded to the suggestion of her uncle.

"So. That's a good thing. Take you a vacation trip to Colombia. But we gonna get rid of all you got left first before you go, that way, he'll see you are for real, and would wanna move forward with business with you on your own. Trust me, once you let him know what's going on with your boyfriend, and show him the story on the internet, he ain't gonna want shit to do with the guy. Hell, he may do you and me both a favor and have him killed! No more worries for you, none for me, and none for Pete," Leroy expressed his greatest wish for the fate of Montell.

If death was to come to Montell, in the mind of Leroy, it would create the best situation. His niece would be the one in direct contact with a Colombian Cartel leader, and she'd be the one getting supplied with all the work, and would have no worries of her boyfriend getting her all caught up in the mess he has going on with himself, nor jeopardizing her life with Pete by not paying all the money he owes him or having some other misfortune happen to where the drug supply would be compromised.

Leroy himself wouldn't have to continue trying to hunt Montell down behind the rape and murder of a pregnant white girl, and the police could then close the case with the death of a main suspect. Also, no problems from Montell would befall on his niece. Lastly, Pete wouldn't have to worry of Montell becoming a government witness and try to bring him down in the process.

"TeeTee, you old enough to know better now. I told you before, you in the big league now. It ain't no backing away from the point of you speaking to, Pete, in his native tongue and him basically putting you in charge of things from the beginning," he worded to Tamron to encourage her more to take on the roll of boss-lady and continue to step up to the plate.

"How you figure, Uncle Leroy?" she asked.

"Because its self-explanatory, TeeTee. *You* was the one to fully communicate to the man in the way he know best, in the Spanish language, and sealing the deal by giving word you and your boyfriend, would pay all y'all owe in that language. You didn't give your word in English, Tee. You gave it in Spanish. Didn't you?"

"You right about that. You got good insight, Uncle Leroy. Good insight," Tamron responded.

The uncle simply smiled and continued on speaking. "TeeTee, keep my words with you and don't let them be lost, ok. That boyfriend of yours, is now 'dead' to you. He's dead! Cut dude all the way off. And when you're face to face with your connect, you be sure to let him know that as well. From this point on, it ain't no more Montell and TeeTee. It's TeeTee and that's it. I'm your *silent* business partner. Repeat after me, okay. From this point on."

"From this point on," Tamron repeated the words of her uncle.

"It ain't no more Montell and Tee Tee," Leroy proceeded.

"It ain't no more Montell and Tee Tee."

"Montell is dead to me," Uncle Leroy stated.

"Montell is dead to me," repeated Tamron.

"Now, tell Uncle Leroy, where you got the rest of the supply put away at? he asked.

"I got smart about things, Uncle Leroy. I ain't no damn fool. I rented a storage space downtown Atlanta, and put it away there, along with some old clothes, furniture, and some other material I could come up with to load the space down with," she revealed.

Her uncle smiled at her again, displaying his one gold crown he has on one of his front teeth. "That's good, TeeTee. That's good. Now, tell me something else, who all you got on your team to help you move the work?" he stated.

"Just me and a couple of my girls. I had mainly been relying on Montell to sell everything. But that's to be no more. One of my girls on the team, I've got to cut her off too," Tamron said.

"Why? What's the problem?"

She paused to think of something good to tell her uncle on why she planned to terminate the work service of one of her friends. She still had not spoke on it and that caused her uncle to ask once more. "Why, TeeTee?"

She lifted her head and looked her uncle in the eyes. "Because that bitch ain't no good, Uncle Leroy," Tamron spat.

The uncle looked on at her in a puzzled way and was about to inquire, but before doing so, Tamron came on out with it.

"The so-called friend I plan to not deal with any longer, had been secretly dealing with my boyfriend behind me back, Uncle Leroy," she said.

He continued to look on at her and hesitated before speaking. Then, he asked," are you sure about that Tee? You got any proof? The reason I say it is because you don't wanna create any enemies which could potentially do you some harm later down the line. You want her to continue to think you don't know shit. And you don't give a fuck. Truthfully, you shouldn't. And besides, the more she feels like you don't know, the less threatened she'll feel. She'll continue to deal with him and he'll continue to use her to go back and forth between him and you, and eventually, she'll lead us straight to him to get his ass out the way for good, TeeTee. Just listen to your uncle on this, ok. But enough on that. What about this Pete guy? You got any contact information directly to him?" Leroy asked.

"No, I don't. Montell has all that. But I could get in contact with him through his people who we had last met up with to get our supply. They'll call him right up for me with no problem," Tamron replied.

"That's good, that's good. But again, we gonna wait until we sell out and you look to re-up again. It'll be perfect timing, TeeTee. Perfect timing," the uncle had said. "Probably around the end of the week, I'll need you to take out maybe five units, the raw stuff. I got one of my guys getting rid of everything. I'll have them meet up with you to get it. And remember, the only person to contact you on that one particular number is me, ok. That's our exclusive line to communicate. He made clear for her to understand.

"Yes Uncle Leroy," she replied. "But Uncle Leroy, back to this issue Montell wanted on. Might I ask, how much do they got on him?" Tamron asked.

"Oh, they got a lot, I tell you. They got a lot, Tee. His fingerprints was all over the house. We know he and the female had a relationship going on. She was pregnant with his baby. There was footage of him entering the home and exiting fast, and a whole lot more. Not only that the large amount of drugs found in the house. They had the same type of tape and wrapping as those you had here when I came by last time. So, I know they belonged to him," Leroy revealed.

Chapter 7

TAMRON dropped her head and begun to cry.

"TeeTee! What the hell ail you, gal! Stop crying and shit, right now! And I mean it, Damn it!" her Uncle Leroy yelled at her loudly in demand.

"I'm so sorry Uncle Leroy. I just love him, that's all. I Love him," she responded.

"What love got to do with it! I told you, you're in a dangerous game now, Tee. Ain't no room for feelings and emotions here baby girl. It's too late for all that. Too damn late! Now lift your head and get yourself together and your uncle will see you later this week, okay. Come here and give me a hug and let me go."

Tamron got to her feet, hugged her uncle, and wiped the tears from her eyes she'd shed for Montell. The uncle exited the back door, got in his car, and left, headed back to work to do more detective investigations. She was left with more than enough to think about, as she went back to her room and laid on her bed to contemplate and release those remaining tears her Uncle Leroy forced her to hold in. As much as she loved Montell and wanted to be with him, to help see him through this situation as she had times in the past, most notably the time he'd served in Federal and state prisons, she knew there was no way to go against the words of her police uncle and be anywhere near the grim reality associated with the fate Montell was destined to suffer.

"There ain't no more Montell and TeeTee. Montell is dead to you." The words of Uncle Leroy sounded off again in her

mind. She looked over at the phone, grabbed it, and then dialed 6-1-1. She was about to change the number and factory reset her phone. Tamron had also intended to deactivate all social media accounts she had, to prevent Montell from getting in contact with her from any angle.

Uncle Leroy say kill any and all contact between Montell and me. It wont serve me any good to keep in touch with him. Besides, that nigga done raped and killed a white girl who was pregnant by him. He a dead man as soon as the police locate him to shoot him themselves. I can't be apart of no shit like that. I'm on top now. And it's been a long time coming. A long time coming, she had thought long and deep to herself.

The only thing Tamron had left to do was to get off all material she had left, get Pete his money, and continue to move out on that note. She had it going on in a major way. Tamron saw herself as a *"queenpin"* in the making on the streets of ATL. A "Boss-Bitch" to be reckoned with, and she knew it. If only those feelings for Montell would go away, and eventually, they had the potential to. But not that day. All she had to do was keep to the words of her uncle and forget all about dude. *"Montell is dead to me."* She repeated her own words to herself. *"Dead to me!"*

One of her cellphones had begun to ring. It was the one she rarely used, the one to the only person who had the number to it and no one else. "That's Uncle Leroy calling. He must forgot to tell me something when he was here," She said to herself in soliloquy.

"Hello Uncle Leroy," she'd answered.

"Hey, TeeTee. As I was thinking just then, I came to the conclusion, it would really be best if you was to go right on ahead and contact your guy down in the other land the 'P' guy. No need to say a name. What's understood don't need to be spoken on. But the reason I say it is, in the event the dead man tried to contact him and put some BS in the game, like you have ran off on him or stole the material from him, then try to put the 'P' guy on you. But once you let the facts be known and assure him you will be the one to deliver all his money, to trust in you to do so, then, he'll become more accepting of your word and wouldn't wanna deal with the other guy, the dead guy, any longer. Also, TeeTee, I would strongly suggest you put it to him in a way which would cause him to feel really threatened by the dead guy, so P and his people, will go on and put him out of his misery, because I'm telling you, he's not gonna last past the point of the police locating him and looking to put the cuffs on him. They gonna cut him down right there on sight. I promise you on that. It was the main reason why I told you to cut all ties to him. He's a dead man,Tee. A dead-man!"

"Okay, Uncle Leroy, I'll be sure to get on top of it today."

"No not today, TeeTee. Get on top of that *now*, baby girl! You got to reach P before he do. Because it ain't no telling what type of bullshit he plan to put out on you. Just go on and hit P's people and let them know you need to reach him. It's urgent. It's very important," Leroy lastly said.

"Okay. I'm on it now, Uncle Leroy," Tamron responded.

"All right."

They ended the call and Tamron immediately pulled up the contacts she had for Angel and Benita on one of the other phones she owned.

Tamron expressed to Angel, she needed to meet up with them that day—that afternoon—so a conference call could be made to Pete immediately. Benita attempted to get Tamron to let her know what was the urgency of the situation? But Tamron had refused to speak on it until she was present and face to face with them to relate matters to Pete. Angel told her to show up at the farm at five so they all may contact Pete.

At the hour she was to be meeting with Angel and his wife Benita, she was pulling up the driveway of the farm in her Honda Accord, the same vehicle she had been driven at the time her and Montell appeared last time to be supplied.

Angel had been taken by surprise to see Tamron came alone and not with Montell.

"Señorita, Tamron, where is Mo?" he asked.

"He wasn't able to make it today. That was the entire reason why I needed to speak with Pete on such short notice. It's because of the situation Montell has gotten accused of," she responded.

"So, tell me this. Is everything ok with the product? And is everything ok with the money Pete is owed?"

"Yes Angel. Everything is ok with both, the supply and the money we owe Pete. Can you just please, get him on video call for me, Angel? That's all I ask. Please," Tamron answered and expressed for Angel to do.

Angel had complied with what Tamron had requested of him and called up Pete on the Skype app. He related all that was going on, and Tamron was present by herself. She'd called on short notice requesting to speak with him. The very first thing Pete asked of Angel had been, was everything ok with the supply and the money he was owed?

Before Angel could respond, Tamron spoke up to answer for herself.

"Yes Pete. Everything is fine with the supply and the money," she'd said, stepping to the forefront of Angel into the screen of the laptop for Pete to see her. She smiled, prompting Pete to do the same. He quickly went back to posing in his serious demeanor and then asked in Spanish," what was the problem?"

Tamron, doing exactly as her Uncle Leroy told her to do, left no stone not turned in relating everything—of course in Spanish—which Pete highly preferred. Especially so, being she knew the language pretty good herself, and no misunderstanding could take place on such serious matter.

Tamron went so far as to show Pete the video footage from the news station she'd saved on her phone, and gave him other information on where to look up any additional reports of the crime and of Montell being a wanted man.

"So you see, Pete," she said," I hold the responsibility of my own at a time like this that the police has put out wanted alerts for my boyfriend, to take all the supply we had, and I hid it in a safe location away from him. Because my life is on the line too, and we had to see to it you got your money. I did at least, and he had too many other problems to concern himself with. So, with that being said, I want you to know, from here on, it will be me to bring your money, and it will be me to be supplied, okay. 'Mo' is no more! He can't be trusted, and he's in too deep of shit to have a man like you continue to do business with him. His life is basically over with. So, just look for me to pay you, me to keep in contact with you, and for me, to be supplied by you, okay," Tamron stated.

Pete looked on at her and smiled satisfyingly. He approved of her honest and bold approach. "Thank you, Señorita for being truthful the way you are. And most importantly, thank you for giving me notice on how I would be paid, and by who. That's a lot of money Mo owes, and equally, that's a lot of trust I put in Mo to have something like this to occur. I do have two last questions for you. First, how soon will I get my money?" he asked.

Tamron replied in a timely fashion. "It will be soon Pete. In two to three weeks. I've got to sell it myself and keep things rolling. So, soon. Okay."

"Fair enough. And my next question to you is, if anything, what would you suggest to be of Mo, if he don't go to prison before I'm to have someone reach him?"

Tamron paused on the last question. It terrified her to death to know that the dude she had absolutely loved, had gotten in too deep and over his head. He couldn't be trusted any longer and Pete was ready to rid himself of the potential threat 'Mo' posed to him. Whatever was to be the words that came out of Tamron's mouth, would ultimately be the decision he would base on them.

She finally answered. "I suggest you terminate any and all contact with him, and leave him to self-destruct. That's what I suggest."

"But Señorita, the thing that worries me the most is, Mo knows my brother, he knows of me, and has been to two separate locations I have my people in place at. As a man, I'm sure he is not going to like the fact of his Señorita being the one to continue in doing business with his former supplier, and not he. This may have a negative effect on how he thinks and possibly would react to the fact," he mentioned to Tamron in expressing his overall view of Montell.

"Well Pete, 'Mo,' can feel how he wanna feel and think as he may. It really do not matter to me. All I know is, I've got to be the one to make things right with you, for him, because I was part of the negotiations from the beginning, and I was the one to seal the deal, not him," she stated to the nodding of the head by Pete in agreement to the point she was making. "So, the truth be said, Pete," she'd continued," whatever decision you make on him, is fine by me. You're the boss," Tamron declared. "You're the boss."

His plot was simple as ever to formulate and put out there for Tamron to speak upon. With the questions he asked of her on Montell, his intent was to know if or not there may be any foul play on behalf of the two—Montell or her. Pete had a funny feeling about it all from the moment she'd begun to let him know what the deal was.

But at the point of reviewing the news clip and seeing other material to know in fact, Mo, had problems with the law, Pete ruled out foul play, and turned his thoughts towards the protection of his product and the worker he had in Tamron. He strongly felt the best course of action to take would be to simply eliminate Mo. And then, all his problems would be solved.

"Once again Señorita, Pete spoke up more," I wanna thank you for being forthcoming and letting me know of the situation. You have been well, and your business shall continue," he lastly stated to her and then gave Angel permission to pass over contact information previously not known by her nor Montell. Tamron was now in first place with Pete between her and Montell. She was good to go.

Chapter 8

RODERICK sent Montell an email and told him to be sure to call ASAP and to let him know what the fuck he had going on. He was back in his hometown of Philly and Montell was closer to him than he knew. Roderick wanted him to reply quickly, so they could at least talk, then Montell may be able to tell the people close to him his side of the story, if the nigga would at least call somebody and talk, so thought Roderick.

Montell's world begun to come crashing down on him in the worst type of way. He didn't want to think too hard on it, because he truly needed to take a moment and sit back to get his head together before he was to loose it. The last thing he needed was to lose his freaking mind and not be able to focus on a way to free himself from the ugly situation at hand he faced.

Okay-okay, first thing first, get in contact with Pete and let him know the situation, Montell thought as he sat all alone in the motel room in Dover, Delaware. He knew if anything, he had to face Pete and tell him something. Rather Pete would want to continue in doing business with a him—a "black man who was wanted by the police for the rape and brutal murder of a white girl"—that's yet to be known. But Montell knew he at least had to get in contact, or else.

He went to Pete's information in his phone and attempted to make a call. The number had been disconnected. He next tried to video call him on Skype. That too had failed. *What the fuck! I know I'm trying the correct numbers. What's going on?* Montell wondered. He gave up trying to contact Pete after several miscues. Montell next tried to contact Angel. He too had either changed or disconnected his numbers. Then next, attempted to call Tamron. No success. *Now I know I ain't going muthafuckin' crazy, am I! How the fuck has everybody number all of sudden gotten changed or disconnected just like that on me?* He had no idea on what to think.

Montell had tried one last number to someone he knew may still have the same contact information and would at least let him know what's going on, why was it that people seem to be switching up on him all of a sudden? It was the number to his friend still on lock in the Feds, Pete's brother, Raul.

Montell texted first:

Yo. Raul. It's me, Montell. You available?

It took Raul about five minutes to reply, but nonetheless, he did so

RAUL: *Sorry about the delay bro. It was count time.*

Montell took a look down at the time on the phone. *Damn! It is count time up in there. I had forgot.*

Raul text a second time.

RAUL: Mo, *hurry up and call me bro. We definitely need to talk, like ASAP!*

Montell then called. Raul answered.

"Mo!"

"Raul! What's up bro. How are you?" he asked.

"I'm maintaining," Raul responded. "But enough with all that. Let's cut the chase. What the fuck you got going on, Reeso?" Raul asked emphatically.

"Damn Raul! How'd you find out so fast bro?" Montell asked of his incarcerated friend.

"It wouldn't take too long, if the friend had been connected to the brother, who is the plug, and the friend owes a half milli, and won't be able to pay the supplier due to being on the run from the cops!" Raul responded.

"Raul. I'm innocent bro. Word on that I'm innocent as can be. I ain't do shit wrong, bro. God be my witness," Montell said.

"That may be so, bro. But according to Pete, you've fucked up big time with him. And now, you got him pissed at me too behind the shit bro."

"I told you, I'm innocent. I tried to call Pete many times but his numbers ain't good no more. What the fuck going on with that? It's why I called you to try and get his new numbers bro," Montell said.

"Reeso. Truth be told bro, my brother ordered me not to even talk to you any longer, that you and your services are no longer needed by us," Raul informed.

"What! How all of a sudden he's now against me? And I *owe* him money?" Montell wanted to know.

"Reeso, for one, you on the run from the police, dawg. For another, you owe me brother money that you not able make, because you're not able to get off the supply to pay him. The police found five kilos of the work at the home of the girlfriend you're being accused of killing. He's afraid of doing any business with you now. And not only that he told me some female of yours, somebody you use to deal with, he only said a 'Señorita,' had assured him *she* would be the one to get rid of the supply and get his money to him," Raul made him aware. Pete said the female told him to do whatever he felt needed to be done to you, if the cops don't get to you first."

There was a pause between the two. *That nasty bitch Tamron! I should've known that bitch would try to cross me out at some point behind the NeNe shit! Dirty bitch!* Montell thought.

Raul continued. "Reeso. I'm sorry bro. Ain't shit I could do to help you. It's out of my hands. It's out of my hands, bro," Raul stated and awaited to see what Montell's reply would be be.

"Yeah alright bro. I get it. I understand man. Just please keep in mind, Raul, I'm innocent. I ain't do the things I'm being accused of. And lastly, if by chance you're able to convince Pete to hear you out in conversation which has my name it, please find a way to get through to him and have him at least hear me out and allow me the opportunity to speak on my own behalf to explain some things to him. My point is, as long as I see to it he gets paid his money I owe him, nothing else should matter other than that."

"Reeso, I'mma say this again for you, dude, ok. Because you don't seem to get it. The-cops-found-five-kilos-of-the-supply-at-the-home of the girl-you-accused-of-killing! I slowly worded it so you'll clearly get it dude! Five kilos of *Pete's* supply! He don't trust you any longer. He never will again, bro. Now, I've got to end this call. And keeping to the oath of my family, I've got to also end this contact and friendship you and I once had. Take care of yourself, Reeso, and I wish you the best of luck," Raul remarked and ended the call promptly between he and Montell.

Montell was left dumbfounded about it all and without any type of answer to the downward progression he'd been experiencing without a doubt. He knew for a fact, Tamron, had crossed him out with Pete. He also had good reason to believe it was no one other than, Tamron, who contacted Pete before he could, and made him aware of the situation he had with the police. But did Tamron really cross him out, or just did the necessary thing to save one of the two in the situation?

He was still busting his brain trying to figure out who it had possibly been to kill Mandy in the way she'd been murdered? The terrible imagines was permanently etched in his mind of how he'd found Mandy, stabbed up and laid out on the floor, in a pool of her own thickened blood. It brought tears to his eyes to know she'd been done in the way she had.

Montell cried and cried to himself. He hadn't been in such state of emotion in years, ever since the early days of him being incarcerated after they all was arrested.

Following a few minutes in tears, he'd gotten himself together and begun to browse through his phone. He noticed he had an email. It was one from Roderick. He left his phone number for Montell to call as well. A different one than he had before.

Montell texted first: *Yo Rod, its me Mo.*

Roderick replied: *Yo nigga. What the fuck is going on with you? I mean you do have friends and business partners out here. I'm calling now.* Roderick declared, then did so.

"What up Rod," Montell answered.

"What the fuck, Mo! How the hell you just up and get ghost on us, and not allow us to help you in your time of need? And how you not mention anything to us on the situation you now going through? We would had rather hear it from you directly, than to have that nigga '*Geno*' telling us about it!" Roderick said.

"Rod, I'm innocent, bro. I ain't do no shit like that and you know it!" Montell responded.

"Mo. What the fuck really happened, dude?" Roderick asked bluntly.

Montell went on to tell him the entire story. Once he'd completed letting Roderick know what the deal really was, Roderick had been able to look at him in a better way than he had prior to.

"So, where you at now, bro?" Roderick asked.

"I'm so far away from Atlanta right now, bro," Montell responded.

"I'm not in Atlanta myself either, bro. I'm back in Philly. Jamie told me the police been hot at the spot and the whole situation with you made it bad for business. He also say that the nigga Geno, ain't quit speaking negative about you since the moment he seen you on the news," Roderick related.

"Man fuck that nigga! I ain't got time to be concerned with no shit like that my nigga. But anyway, I'm in Delaware, bro."

"Oh you in Delaware?"

"Yeah. I've been laying low bro."

"Maybe sometime soon you can come up here to Philly until you get things in order and be able to hire a lawyer to fight it out of this situation you in now."

"Yeah Rod, I definitely would be up for that. Philly got more size to it than do Dover, so, I should be able to move about a little better. I drove my car too, so everything will be fine on transportation," Montell mentioned to this friend.

"Good bro. Good. But no matter what, you already know me and Jamie got your back all the way through this," Roderick assured.

"That's real bro. I just hate the fact this happen, and especially so with the police finding my money and the other shit I had there at her house. It only makes it tougher for me to try and prove I ain't have nothing to do with her being killed. Hopefully, they collected some type of DNA or other evidence that's gonna get me from under being a suspect," Montell had expressed.

"I hope so too, bro. But anyway, you got my number here, and thankfully, you didn't delete your email account and I was able to reach you like I have."

"Yeah bro, I'm here."

"More than likely, I'd probably wanna take a ride up your way this weekend, and we could come together and do some things," Montell mentioned to Roderick.

"Sounds like a plan, Mo. Just get at me."

"I'll do that Rod."

"Okay, you be easy, Montell. And I'll see you soon." Roderick lastly spoke. They ended the call.

Montell begun to brainstorm yet again in trying to think of any way he could on how he might he able to get back in contact with Tamron, and have her to give him back his drug supply so he could get back to hustling and making some money. He had to come up with a way to generate a flow of income and get things going again. His predicament was a tough one to be in, but nonetheless, he knew he had to do something, because the twenty thousand he had would only last so long.

Roderick texted again. There was something he was meaning to have brought to Montell's attention, but had forgot. Roderick let him know, the upcoming Monday, would be the day he and Lea had to appear at court and would definitely see Eric there. He knew it would be news Montell would want to hear. If only he didn't have the type of warrant out for his arrest as he had, he'd more than likely take the risk to be present.

Chapter 9

Verena had finally made up her mind. She was completely done with Eric on all levels. Completely done with him, so she thought to herself. Ever since their last fight and break-up, he hadn't called, he hadn't asked how was the kids, nor made any contact with Verena. He had contemplated not appearing to court on those charges he and Joleena caught, but stopped short of doing so behind the thought of such action not being good for business, as he'd gotten closer to Joleena's brother Robert, and things was looking upward for them in a lot of areas.

Verena wanted to see Eric and possibly have a few words with him as it was the day he was to appear before the judge to face the charges from the Atlantic City incident. She also had in mind to finally find out what the Mexican female looked like who had taken her man from her.

The hearing was scheduled for ten that morning. Verena was there at nine, so as to observe Eric, Joleena, and the people who they'd got to fighting with.

At nine forty-five A.M, Eric and Joleena were pulling into the parking lot. The couple got out the car, grabbed hold of one another hands and begun to make way to enter the courtroom. Halfway across the parking lot, their path had been cut off by Verena.

"So how you been doing, Eric. Huh! You do know you got a woman and two kids at home, don't you!"

"Verena, please, ok. Not today. Not now. I'm already trying to get out the mess I'm in and you wanna bring more drama my way. Why?" responded Eric.

"DRAMA! So I'm bring drama your way now? You leave me and our twin babies at home, and I'm drama?" Spat Verena.

"Okay-okay-okay. Wait. What!" Joleena spoke out. "You have a girlfriend at home and a set of twins, Eric?" she asked him, as she pulled her hand away from his, looked on at him, and awaited him to provide some type of answers.

Verena answered for him. "Yes! He does! And by the way, who are you?" she questioned Joleena.

"I am his *main* girlfriend. The one whose been by his side for the past weeks leading up to this day. The one who rubs his back, cooks his food, and pleases him the way he loves to be pleased. The one brings peace to his life and not the drama like you have done. That's who I am," Joleena spoke up to Verena.

Verena really didn't know how to reply to the words of her now female nemesis, the one she would have to battle with over Eric. She just stood and looked on at Joleena, and her hand propped on her hip, not really looking to continue on in argument.

"Look Eric, I only came here because of course, I had to post your bail on these charges, my name is on the bond documents, and I needed to speak with you about our babies. That's all. Hopefully, you're man enough to do that? Hopefully," Verena said.

"Eric!" Joleena spoke louder to gain his full attention. "Why you never told me you have children? You mentioned about a girlfriend you was trying to leave, but nothing about the two of you having kids. This ain't right, Eric. Now you got your kids caught between your troubles."

"Joleena, look sweetie. It's not that serious, okay," Eric said.

"It's not that serious! It's not that serious! Me and our babies are not that serious now, huh!" Verena blurted.

"Verena, look. Please, ok. Truth be I've fallen for Joleena—"

"And exactly *who* is she above me?" Verena asked sarcastically.

Eric did the wise thing in such moment and not say a word. At least not in response to Verena.

"Joleena, sweetie, I was gonna tell you of my kids eventually," Eric said.

"As a woman, Eric, I have to take into account how she may feel about you walking out on her and the two kids you both have together. That's just not right," Joleena expressed how she felt about him not telling her of the kids he had.

"Joleena, my intent was to make you aware—"

"Just be easy, Eric. We could talk about it later, okay. Let's go in and deal with this first."

Verena only looked on at them and had a final word to Eric before they were to enter the courtroom. That makes two conversations you got to have, now don't it!"

Once inside the courtroom and seated, no one spoke on the relationship issues anymore. The three just kept quiet. Verena sat in a seat one row behind Eric and Joleena. Five minutes later, the two siblings entered. Roderick and Lea, looked at Eric and his Spanish girlfriend with mean-mugs and cold stares, as they occupied seats across the aisle. Verena took notice of the ugly attitude and nature the two displayed towards Eric and Joleena. She'd seen photos of Roderick from times in the past when she was warden and recognized his face.

Wait a minutes. That's Eric's friend Roderick, ain't it? Or his use to be friend. Is he the one Eric got to fighting with? Probably so, she thought. Then, it hit her. The report from the newspaper, Roderick was the one Eric was fighting with. Let me, just sit back and see what's going on with this here, Verena further thought.

The hearing begun and the judge read off the names of the people who had to appear, the charges faced, and the actions which could be taken to have the charges taken care of or answered to by some form of punishment. The formalities of court proceedings, so to speak.

All the fines and other court fees had been paid off by everyone, and the cases were closed. They exited and had a few words to say to one another before they got in their vehicles to leave.

Roderick spoke out first,"Yo Eric. Ol' lame-ass nigga! Ain't tha's the bitch Verena you ran off with on Montell and us? Taking all of our money in the process?" he reminded.

Eric, flushed with anger, at the thought of all the money of his Verena still had.

"Yeah, that's the bitch! I want my motherfucking money you and this bitch-ass nigga of yours have stolen! You got that!" Roderick pointed his finger and spat angrily at Verena.

"Don't look to me for nothing. There's your guy right there to be pissed with," Verena muttered and pointed to Eric. "It was all his idea," she added.

"And yours too, bitch! Stop trying to be slick!"

Verena snarled at Roderick behind his disrespect in words.

"Yo sis, come on. Let's go before we fuck up and catch more charges behind beating this nigga's ass and both his bitches!" Roderick insulted and he lead the way to his car parked across the lot from Eric's ride and Verena's Cadillac, the vehicle she paid for with the money from the tax scam.

Once Roderick and Lea took a seat, they lay back and looked at Eric and his two women, as the potential of some additional drama loomed. Roderick was really determined to get the tag numbers of both vehicles of them, Eric and Verena. His intent was to kill two birds with one stone, and deal with them both at the same time, as he had punishment exacted on their heads for the high level of violations the two committed by taking their money, Montell and crew, including his.

"Lea, pay attention to the cars they get in and snap a few pictures of them and the license plates, okay," he instructed his sister.

"Got you bro. I'm on it."

"So Eric, this what I'm going to do, because Lord knows, I don't want to continue to argue with you or go back and forth about you not wanting to be home with me and our kids, and you'd rather go on in life as a deadbeat. Listen and listen well, okay. If you, get your ass in that car and ride off on me and my babies, leaving me to raise them by myself while you and that (she lifted her hand to give gesture at Joleena) ride off into the sunset to live life together happily ever after, I can promise you, you will pay! I promise you on that!"

"Oh yeah. What you gone do, Rena? Huh! What do you actually got in mind? Eric responded.

"You really wanna know?"

"I asked didn't I," Eric spat sarcastically.

"I'mma give you an ultimatum, okay. Here it is. You can come on follow me to our home where our babies are, and we work this out for the better, and not go through this again. Or else, there will be hell to pay, and else more," Verena declared.

"Sounds like one helluva ultimatum to me. Now, or else what?" Eric challenged.

"Or else, I'm gonna call the IRS on you, him (she pointed towards Roderick's direction), Montell, and Jamie; and report y'all asses behind the tax scams y'all did. And I can provide names, dates, and all else that the bastard Montell had stole out my office for y'all to do, the information of those other inmates whose identity he'd stolen, and everything else. Now try me if you think I'm playing!" Verena threatened. She had tears in her eyes at this point.

Eric couldn't believe his fucking ears. "Did this bitch just threaten to fucking snitch on me to the IRS? I know damn well Verena ain't just say some shit like that to me. Oh, hell fuck nawl! This bitch done lost her mind, haven't she," he said to Joleena, as he looked on at Verena with his mouth wide and an angry disposition cast over his face.

It took him some time to respond to her, but reluctantly, he finally did. "Verena, you see, now you've gone too far. You just went too far!" he said.

"Okay, and what have you done? You don't think you've went too far yourself, Leaving me and my babies by ourselves?" she retorted.

Eric only looked at her eye-to-eye and shook his head. "She got to be flexing on me. Ain't no way she'd do that. She had everything to do with it too, and she'd run the risk of getting herself caught up if she did what she's now threatened to do," he informed Joleena.

Verena continued to looked Eric in the eyes and awaited his reply to all she'd said with the ultimatum she'd given him. Joleena didn't know what to say or do. She simply looked on at Eric and Verena herself, as they sparred with their tongues against each other. Finally, he addressed her on the ultimatum given.

"I don't think you stupid enough to do that because it'll implicate you was in on it as well. So, go right on ahead. Do what you got to do. You not gonna force me to be in a relationship I don't want nothing to do with any longer. I plan to live life with the woman I'm with now (he leaned in to kiss Jolina), my sweetie, Joleena," he let out with a smile.

Verena had a very hard time controlling her impulse which was almost caused her to lash out and hit Eric. But she maintained her composure and just stood in one place while absorbing the emotional pain Eric had caused. The tears begun to flow heavily as Eric turned to lead Joleena to the car, opened the door for her—something he'd never done for Verena—allowed her to get in, closed it behind her, walked to the driver side without so much as glanced in Verena's direction, got in his car, and pulled off.

Verena slowly walked to her car—tears still streaming—got in and drove off. Roderick and Lea saw the entire fiasco at a distance. They laughed like hell in the aftermath of the drama. It was a sight to see for them.

Chapter 10

Tamron's Uncle Leroy, had been extra busy ensuring he'd get rid of all the supply she'd passed over to him. He had three other dirty cops who worked for him, and they had people on the street to deal their drugs. It was how their operation was conducted. In a matter of two weeks, he had moved almost the entirety of what Tamron had left to serve. She was down to only four kilos of meth and one of Molly. All of the pills were gone. The people Leroy distributed the drugs to, was spread across the inner city of Atlanta and three other states, Tennessee, South Carolina, and Florida. In wholesale, he sold no less than five kilos at a time, and no one could do business with him if they didn't have $100K or better.

Tamron and her girls made power moves themselves. She didn't have the type of twenty-four hour protection necessary to strictly sell bricks of the work like her uncle did. But as long as they pumped the narcotics out in the way which he did, there wasn't a need for her to do so much.

She and her girls sold ounces at a rapid pace. But the pills, they knocked off at the rate of 100 at a time. They dubbed themselves the "Grade A Clique"—Tamron, Kay-Kay, Nene, Princess, and Pooh. For the most part, everybody but Kay-Kay dealt their own work. Kay-Kay's man, Black Tony, sold most of the material she had.

Leroy met up with his niece to discuss the business they had going on.

"So TeeTee, you say we only down to five of everything right?" he asked.

"That's correct Uncle Leroy."

"Okay. That's beautiful there. That's beautiful. And you owe how much to Pete for your boyfriend?" he asked another question to be sure he had it correct.

"A half million," Tamron replied.

"I'm sure we got that by now, right?"

"We do. And some. On the last re-up, we had just over three hundred thousand of our own money, along with the money we made out the first batch, from the twenty. So now, Pete's money is in place, and I've got three hundred and seventy-five grand between me and my girls, and whatever you plan to put in," Tamron said.

"TeeTee," Leroy said and then slightly chuckled at his niece. "You got a direct line to a Colombian cartel leader, baby girl. All you got to do is prove to him you can handle all he supply you with, and have his money paid on time. That's it! I'm more than sure once you pay Pete off and keep the business clean like it is, he's going to drop more on you, probably more than you had the last time. You don't have that boyfriend around any longer to complicate things for you, and now, you can move on up in a more progressive way. You got me and I've got my team of people, and that's all we need. But here is what I want you to do."

"What's that Uncle Leroy?"

"Look, you tell Pete, once you have to pay him this time, you would like to fly down to Colombia to meet him, and you two have a sit down to discuss more business. In the phone call to him, you be sure to let him know you don't want any more supply at the moment, until after you and him have met, in Colombia. The trick is to let him get a personal observation of you, on his home turf, and to allow him the chance to directly lay out the terms on how things are to go from that point forward. I promise you, he's gonna lay so much on you from there, you and I will be able to make a fortune. Also, once you two do talk, and he recognize your level of maturity and how serious you've become from times before, he'll clearly know, yes, you have someone behind you other than your boyfriend whose leading and coaching you the right way. Trust me on this," Tamron's Uncle Leroy said to her.

At the mention of the word "boyfriend," it triggered the feelings and emotions inside of her she felt for Montell, and that in a sense, caused her to miss him and long for the days of their past.

A down cast look came about her face, as she wished like crazy she was in a better position to help him out. But unfortunately, she wasn't, and all which they had was no more.

Chapter 11

Tamron finally responded to all her uncle said to her. "I clearly understand you well. I know if anyone, you are the one best suited to give me advice on how this is to go and on how I should go about doing it. Everything you just told me to do, I plan to do so. Good things are sure to line up for me, I strongly believe," Tamron said.

"Okay. Fine. Now that we have that part out the way, I've got a little update on your boyfriend's situation. The APD has been in close contact with the Georgia Bureau of Investigations ("GBI") relating to this case. Sure enough, they have an ass of evidence against Mister Montell McNeal... to put his ass away forever! And when I say 'forever,' I mean, just that forever! We raided the apartment he was living in looking for him. We even went down to the 'strip club' he got smart enough to put under his step dad's name, trying to locate him. He's nowhere to be found, To sum it up, he's no longer wanted for questioning. We now want him for the crimes themselves! So, whatever you do, TeeTee, do not have any contact with that guy, okay. DO NOT! And your uncle mean that. Now let me go and you be sure to go ahead and contact Pete to let him know you have his money, and let him know everything else you got in mind to do. You take care and I'll be looking for you to get back with me soon, okay baby girl. Oh Yeah. I almost forgot, Landy asked about you the other day," Leroy said to Tamron.

"Oh she did. How is she? How is life for her up in New York?" Tamron asked about her cousin, Leroy's daughter she grew up with.

"She, the baby, and her husband are well. They plan to come down to visit on Thanksgiving. I'll be sure to give her your new number."

"Please do Uncle Leroy. I haven't spoken to her in a long time. We got a lot to catch up on," Tamron lastly said.

"Okay, I'm gone TeeTee. Take care."

"You too Uncle Leroy." And the meeting between uncle and niece drug dealers came to an end.

***

Tamron contacted Angel and let him know she would be on the way with Pete's money later in the day and asked he go ahead and call up the cartel leader and major supplier on U.S. soil, to let him know what the business was, and she really wanted to speak with him on something else related to the business moving forward. Angel agreed to do so and lastly let her know, he'll be awaiting her presence.

The phone call between them ended on that note. She then got busy packing the rolls of money into her tote bag, on by Gucci.

Later that evening, about seven thirty, she was pulling into the driveway of Angel's farm. He and his wife, Benita, was awaiting, as Tamron texted upon first pulling in.

"Hello, Señorita. How are you?"

"Yes. How are you, Miss Tamron."

The husband and wife both greeted.

"I'm well, wonderful people. I am well," she responded.

"Please, come inside and let's get down to business, shall we?" Angel urged.

"As we shall," stated Tamron in remark as she exited her Honda and grabbed the handles of the tote. They all stepped into the house and went to the dining room. Business had begun.

"Here is Pete's money. It's all there," stated Tamron. Angel opened the tote, observed all the currency inside, zipped it back closed, and passed to Benita. She went to the bedroom with it and remained there to allow the two to talk.

Angel called up Pete on Skype and the conference call between the three was in session.

"Senór, we have all of your money," Acknowledged Angel.

"Very well. Very well. I thank you Senórita, for doing the right thing and taking care of the affairs of your boyfriend," said Pete.

"Former boyfriend, Pete. We no longer together. As you already know, he's in too much trouble for me," responded Tamron.

"Okay. Former boyfriend," Pete replied and immediately went into the Spanish language.

Tamron expressed her desire to travel to Colombia for a sit down with Pete. He was very skeptical at first, but then, he agreed, because he respected her ambition and drive. Indeed, he'd had many personal sit downs with men who he supplied, but never a female. Tamron would be the first. She was sure to let him know all she had left and what would be expected once she returned to the states from Medellin. Pete advised she schedule the trip to be in two weeks from the day. She agreed.

The conference call ended and Tamron had been in the process of leaving. As she excited the door, she stopped, turned to face Angel, and said to him," damn Angel. I almost forgot. Tell Benita I need that bag back. It mean something to me."

Montell had bought it for her on her birthday. She loved that Gucci bag.

Chapter 12

Geno found the situation Montell was in to be one he could utilize to his benefit and capitalize from in his quest to strong arm the rights and deeds to full ownership of Seduction City. With him out the way, and Roderick going with the flow on whatever, Geno knew it would be nothing from that point to move Jamie to see things in the way he did.

Geno had gotten power hungry, and hell bent on getting it. He went to his uncle Felix's house and the two talked over some things.

"So unc, look, the nigga Montell, has gotten himself in a mess with the police and really don't have a way out. He's fucked! His part of the club is really available for one of us to obtain," Geno expressed and gestures back and forth between he and Felix.

"I see. Damned fool done fucking raped and killed a white gal! And fucked up by leaving five keys of dope along with money in the house. Now how crazy was that!" Felix responded.

"Shit. Tell me about it. As I said, the nigga is fucked! Raw with no grease either!" Geno sarcastically remarked. "But on the business side of things, something has got to be done with his part. And fast unc," Interjected Geno. He continued. "The Atlanta Police and the GBI has come by twice looking for dude. That ain't good for business!"

"No. It ain't. Not good at all. And at the same time, his part of the club under his stepdad's name, and he don't even live in Atlanta. Before we know it, the police will be busy trying to tie drug money from him to the ownership of the club, since they found drugs at the crime scene too," Felix expressed his concern.

And see, that's my point unc. We running the risk of having the fucking authorities coming and taking our shit, due to that nigga still having something to do with it. I ain't gonna have that shit, uncle Felix. We got to get the nigga out the way now, before its too late," Geno revealed his thoughts to Felix.

"You talk to Jamie about any of this yet?"

"What the fuck I need to talk to that nigga about? I didn't see the need to. If anything, he should be thinking in the same way we are, to cut all ties with that hot-ass nigga Montell!" he said and paused to allow his uncle to speak.

Felix didn't speak fast enough for Geno, so, he continued to talk.

"Unc. Man, fuck them niggaz! Seduction City your shit! It belong to you, and you put me over it! What the fuck we say, is what goes! Period! We run Seduction City. Just like BMF ran the 'A' in our day. Besides, Jamie should be thinking like we thinking and trying to move that nigga out the way," Geno spat.

"That's definitely understood, nephew. But from a business perspective, I still say we should talk with Jamie before we pull the plug on Montell and his part of SC," Felix said.

"Unc. Listen to yourself man. If anything, like I said, Jamie should already be aiming to cut that nigga loose and be done with him. You know what. Better yet, let me talk to Jamie. I got that nigga seeing shit my way any-how, so, don't worry about him. In the next couple of days, Jamie will more than likely be getting in touch with you to tell you to go ahead and move dude out the way. One thing I know about Jamie, is, he all about business and having no confrontation," Geno said.

"That do sounds like Jamie. But here's the thing, Geno. What if the money Montell put in gets brought up?" Felix asked.

"Unc, from what I know, that nigga not gonna be able to spend nothing but seventy dollars a week on the store in the Georgia prison system! He should be good! Those few little pennies he invested is not gonna be missed. I promise you," Geno said.

"Do what you got to do, nephew. It's on you over there. Felix said in response.

"That's all I needed to know, unc. That's all I needed to know," said Geno, and they concluded the conversation and topic related to Montell.

The plan Geno had in mind was to strong arm everybody at SC out of their rights of ownership and be the sole owner himself, and then, he could move on up in the world as a business mogul on the surface and a drug lord on the low. He was making power grabs and major moves one play at a time, as he was desperate to be at the top.

Chapter 13

Verena kept true to her word. She'd contacted the IRS and reported Eric, Montell, Jamie, and Roderick. A detailed account of the actions of the crew had been provided to the government. The dirty bitch let them know she was the warden of the prison in Georgia at the time, and that the inmate/orderly—"Montell Jermaine McNeal"—had stolen a cellphone from her desk; had printed out the information of multiple inmates; and he, along with the other three, put together a major in income tax scam and other fraudulent schemes from the information of those other inmates.

She contacted the Georgia Department of Corrections and requested a roster off all the inmates at the prison for the months she knew the scams was being performed. Verena faxed the list of names to the IRS for them to investigate.

"I got myself caught up with you, but now, it's all over. I reported you and your boys to the IRS, motherfucker! They'll be coming to pick you up soon. And don't worry about trying to stop by this house any longer attempting to see my babies. I have a restraining order on you as well!" Verena let Eric know upon calling him.

"It's all good. It's all good Verena. Now I know for a fact I did the right thing by leaving your fat-ass for a woman that's way better than you'll ever be! Looks or otherwise! You're nothing to me, you sorry ass wanna be high class bitch—"

"HUSH! Don't you talk to me like that! You should know better! And your little Mexican peasant you got for a girlfriend don't have nothing on me as a woman! Nothing!" Verena defended.

"I bet her sex better than yours, and she don't take me through any bullshit like you have. I'm happy what we had is over with. You're not worth the headache, sweetie," Eric said and abruptly ended the call.

Verena attempted to call back to argue and taunt more, but Eric had powered his phone off on her.

In Verena's mind, the IRS would be immediately sending enforcement to arrest Eric and the others, due to the accuracy and detailing of all she'd told. But things didn't simply work that way. An investigation had to be conducted, and other due process procedures had to be followed before any arrest could be made. She wanted Eric off the streets and out of her way.

Verena was a devastated woman behind the fact her and Eric was no more, as he'd gotten very strongly involved with someone else, someone much younger and more appealing than she. Verena never fathomed the thought of things coming to an end between them in such type of way. She'd been beaten by him, she felt used, and the relationship had been long abandoned by Eric. Atop of that the neglect of the twins which he'd done couldn't be made up for on no end. The more and more Verena thought of how terrible things had become for her and Eric, the more she cried to herself, as he was the only dude she ever had intentions to marry.

Her mind shifted back to the day they'd first heard one anothers voice over the phone, and the day they met at Lenox Square Mall to only exchange money from his possession to hers, but turned into a five-hour date over a meal and ice cream . . .

***

Next beside Verena on the nightstand sat a large bottle of wine she'd gotten from Eric's man cave in the basement, and a family size bottle of prescription sleeping pills. Verena felt horrible and was completely down in her level of self-confidence and emotions. Her life was coming to an end, she felt, and no need to continue living life, if she didn't have her dear Eric to live it with.

She'd turned suicidal in conscience and suffered dramatically from the thoughts thereof. The top of the pill bottle had been twisted off and she dumped twelve or more of the powerful sleep-inducing agents into her palm, then tossed them to the back of her throat. With her other hand she lifted the wine from the table and took a gulping swig to wash down the pills and let the bottle of wine slide from her grip down to her thigh, taking a bounce, then to the floor the bottle went, spilling alcohol on the carpet.

Verena's intent was to call Tiffany once the exchange of words was over between her and Eric. She hit the icon for contacts on her phone to call her best friend in the nick of time before the medication kicked in to slow her down and eventually put her out in a long deep sleep, possibly the last.

"Hello," Tiffany answered.

In a slurred and drowsy way, Verena's words were unintelligible speech to Tiffany through the phone, something to the effect of "Tiffany. Tiff. It's over between us, girl. He left me."

"Verena. Are you okay?" Tiffany asked. "What's going on with you?"

In her strongest breath, she was able to clearly make a few words understood.

"Tiffany ... Eric ... he left me. I don't want to live no more. I hate myself," she said.

"Wait. Say what Verena! You hate yourself and you don't want to live anymore? Is that what you said?" Tiffany reworded questioningly.

"I'm about to kill myself," Verena lastly said before blacking out.

"Verena! Verena! You there? Talk to me please. Verena," Tiffany called out for her to respond.

Tiffany immediately called Verena's mother and told her all Verena had said.

"Miss Deanne! Something going on with Verena. Something not right!" Tiffany said

Mrs. Deanne was at her sister's house not too far away with the twins. Verena dropped them off there for the day and returned home in the hopes to have a decent conversation with Eric and possibly convince him to come by the house for them to talk face to face and maybe make up with fantastic sex. But that didn't happen, none of it. Not anywhere near how she planned it from the moment Eric answered with a harsh tone of voice.

Chapter 14

Mrs. Deanne questioned what was going on.

"Miss Deanne, Rena said something about Eric leaving her, she hated herself, and she was about to kill herself! You need to call her and see what's going on. She was talking but then the phone got quiet. I don't know what's going on," Tiffany said.

"I'll call you back shortly, Tiffany. Let me call her now to know what she got going on," Mrs. Deanne said and ended the call with Tiffany to call her daughter. Verena's phone simply continued to ring, then go to voicemail. Mrs. Deanne tried five times but got no answer from Verena. She next dialed 9-1-1 and reported to the police and asked for them to go to their residence and check the situation out.

The cops made it to residence in less than ten minutes. They made repeated attempts to get someone to answer the front door but was unsuccessful. Mrs. Deanne was on the phone with the 9-1-1 dispatcher at the same time the police were banging on the front door of the house.

"There's a spare key hid under one of the flowerpots in front of the house, 'the purple pot,'" Mrs. Deanne informed.

The police located the key, unlocked the door, entered the home, and found Verena dangerously near the point of being unresponsive. Paramedics were called for and she was transported to the hospital to have her stomach pumped and further treated. She was in a state of being in a light coma.

Mrs. Deanne, her sister, and the husband of the sibling, went to the hospital to see how Verena had been doing following her attempt to kill herself. Mrs. Deanne absolutely could not believe Verena would do such a thing. But you just never know what's on a person's mind in those type of domestic circumstances.

She called Eric and tried to get down to the problems which plagued the relationship he and her daughter had. He didn't have any answers for Mrs. Deanne. All he continued to say was, he doesn't know what had gotten into Verena, he simply doesn't know.

Chapter 15

Three Days Later...

Tiffany was on a plane from Atlanta to New Jersey to check on her best friend. Verena had begun to come out of the state she was in, and had her eyes open but not talking. A security guard was on hand to monitor Verena as well. Little did she know, once the treatment was complete, by law, Verena would be involuntarily admitted into a mental health institution for a time being, until a judge makes a determination she's no longer a danger to herself nor to others. There was no time frame on how long the evaluation could take, and Verena would have to remain a patient and receive treatment the entire time at the state hospital.

***

"I knew that silly bitch was crazy! I knew it!" Eric said in soliloquy. *I'm so glad I made the move I had at the appropriate time, long before the dizzy bitch would had nutted up on me! Now I know I did the right thing.* Eric thought.

"Joleena, you won't believe this shit, sweetie," he said to the new girlfriend.

"And what is it babe?" Joleena responded.

"How about, my ex-girlfriend now in the hospital for trying to kill herself on an overdose of pills baby?"

"Say what. Noooo Eric. How could she do such a thing? Why would she do such a thing and she got babies that's not even a year in age yet?" Joleena questioned.

"Beats the hell out of me babe. I don't know. All I do know is, I'm happy to have brought things to an end between us the way I did and in the nick of time I had. Who knows, the crazy-bitch probably would've tried to poison and kill me too," Eric expressed.

"Eric, don't say that about your kid's mother. That's rude bae."

"What! It's the truth, sweetie. She is a crazy and mentally unstable woman. Now, I've got to try to get my kids from her before the state gets them. Miss Deanne, her mother, is too old to be running after and trying to raise kids. The DFACS people are not gonna deem Verena a safe and stable parent any longer, and they will more than likely try to take custody of my kids. I can't allow that."

"No, Eric, we can't allow that baby. I'm now with you, and their livelihood is with me too," Joleena said and leaned in to kiss Eric as they sat on the couch in the living room of his home.

Chapter 16

Eric had a few things to worry about in addition of how he was to take full custody of his kids. He knew without a doubt Verena had in fact called the IRS on him and his old crew. Her threats were real. He felt the possibility existed indeed, they would investigate and may discover something to have them indicted. Something had to be done to prevent the kids from entering Children and Youth. The worst thing that could happen for him was if he was going through the process for custody of the twins and ended up getting arrested in the proceedings of court. Being arrested period was the last thing he could think, which would bring further harm than already occurring. He could have his mother or his sister do whatever necessary to have custody. At all cost something had to be done, and fast!

***

Tiffany was by Verena's side from the time she recovered in the hospital and was released to the authorities to be taken to a mental asylum. Mrs. Deanne pleaded with Tiffany to take custody of the kids in the event the state would try to snatch them away from her. Tiffany agreed, but was sure to add, it would be temporary, due to the things she had going on in her own personal life.

For her to properly assume the role as guardian of the twins, Tiffany would need to move to New Jersey from Georgia, a move she had no problem with. The thing was, she was still in contact with Montell and vowed to help him out of the ordeal he found himself going through. She didn't know he was in the north himself and had thought him to be down in Georgia still, in his hometown city of Albany.

The last she knew, he was only wanted for questioning, and he'd mention clearing his name. But Montell had deeper, more troubling woes which loomed over his head in two major ways. One; with the police and the issue of Mandy's murder; and two, with Pete, possibly gunning for his head, now out of fear Montell may squeal to the Feds on all he knew of his operations. Montell was in a mess.

He hit Tiffany up on the phone one day, as she was still in New Jersey getting the affairs of her friend in order for her.

"Hello. This is Tiffany," she answered the strange number which showed in her caller ID with a 267-area code.

"Hey. Tiffany. How are you?" Montell greeted.

"I'm fine. Who is this?" she wanted to know, as she didn't recognize Montell's voice so readily.

"It's me, Montell," he said in a whisper.

"Hey. Everything fine with you?"

"Yeah. It is. I went to the police like I told you I would in our very brief conversation, and cleared my name. I'm good now," Montell lied.

"That's very good to know. I'm up north in Jersey for the time being," Tiffany revealed.

"Oh. You are. You must be attending something Verena got going on?"

Damn! I forgot Montell and Verena had something going on at one particular time. Tiffany thought.

"Well it didn't take you long to figure that out. Yeah, that's what I'm doing. But it's not what you may think. In fact, it ain't nothing good at all, Montell. Tiffany informed.

"What's going on now, Tiff?" he had asked.

She had sighed in exhale before thinking of the best way to relate bad news to a former boyfriend of her lifelong friend. Without any further delay, she begun to tell Montell what the situation was.

"Montell, listen, okay? Things have not been so good for Verena with Eric or in life. And the only reason I intend to mention any of this to you is due to the fact of me knowing you mean well and you only want the best for Verena, even though she did you wrong. It also wouldn't hurt that I need someone to talk to, and you and I are acquainted some type of way," Tiffany expressed.

"Right-Right-Right on that Tiff. But I'm listening though. Go right on ahead, okay," Montell responded.

"Verena tried to commit suicide, Montell," she blurted.

"SAY WHAT! How did it come to that with her?" he questioned. Things took a turn for the worse between her and Eric. He ditched her and the twins, and the life they were to have lived together," Tiffany revealed.

"Nooo! I honestly can't believe I'm hearing this," he responded.

"Yep. You are. It's true."

"How exactly did she try to do herself?" Montell had the gall to ask.

"She O-D'ed on pills. Thankfully she thought to give me a call at the very moment she had ended her call with Eric, and I had to hurry and contact her mother for her to make it to the house to check on her. But Miss Deanne thought to call the cops would be best, which turned out to be the better judgment. It saved her daughter's life," she had said.

"So, what now?" Montell questioned in a fawning manner to know the full details of all which was to go on from that point, as if he truly cared for Verena and her problems.

"Well, I'm gonna have temporary custody of the kids until they free Rena from the state hospital. A judge has ordered her to remain for a time being."

"DAMN! This is serious ain't it," worded Montell.

"Hell yeah it is," replied Tiffany.

"And then what?" he further asked.

"I've got to take care of things for her until she is capable of doing so herself again."

"You always was the most caring friend Verena had," Montell stated to encourage Tiffany further.

"Well, I thank you, Montell," she said in a way to imply to him to change the subject. He was able to comprehend and did so of his own accord.

"So, you say you're in Jersey now huh?" he asked for clarity.

"Yes, I am. And what about you? Back in Atlanta or still down in Albany?" Tiffany asked.

"Actually, I'm up north too. I'm in Philly," Montell revealed.

"Oh. That's good to know. That's a better place to be than down there anyway. Especially so once you was able to clear your name and relieve yourself of potential trouble. That's definitely something you do not need, ... trouble," Stated Tiffany.

"You're damn sure right about that. Damn sure right about that. Since were close, I was in the hopes we could meet up someday," Montell suggested.

"That might be a possibility. How long will you be in Philly?" She'd asked.

"I plan to stay for a time being. At least six months to a year. You know how the old saying goes, out of sight, out of mind. The further I'm away from the situation down South, the better it is for me. I absolutely don't need them trying to question me any further or attempting to implicate me no type of way."

"That was the smart thing to do, Montell. Get the farthest away from them as possible, long before they try to plant something on you and frame you."

"Hell yeah it was," Montell commented behind Tiffany's words.

Chapter 17

They continued to talk a little longer and made plans to meet up at some point in the next ten days. Montell had in mind to keep Tiffany in the blind about the grim reality of his overall situation as best he could and utilized her to his advantage until things was to improve. He also could get her to provide him with as much information unknowingly about Verena as possible, to aid him in speeding up the process of Verena's eventual downfall, atop of the crisis she now dealt with. If Eric would've been included in the woes on a level as is Verena, Montell would have begun to experience a degree of relief from what both had done to him. He'd have a deeper satisfaction about them being in a terrible predicament together, being they both had snaked him and the others. But hey, Montell was happy to take his victories however they came, and especially so with the problems he had. Any win was a plus in his book. Any win.

***

Montell tilted his head back and let out of sigh of absolute pleasure, as he'd reached his climax and let go of a thick robust load into the mouth of Nene. She had been sucking him off the entire time he'd been talking on the phone with Tiffany. "Ahhh, shit. Hell yeah, girl. Damn that felt so good. I damn sho' love the way you pull on this dick I'm holding, with those pretty lips of yours," Montell complimented.

Nene swallowed his cum, locked eyes with him, blew him a kiss, then continued to clean him up properly. She went back down on him and begun to put in more work, trying to bring him to the top yet again before they were to fuck later on. They were hooked on one another sexually like no other. It was the main reason why he'd sent for her to come to Delaware to begin with. To provide him the pleasure he'd become infatuated with.

Two

Chapter 18

Two Weeks Later...

Months had passed and a lot had happened since they'd last laid eyes on one another physically, and Montell and Tiffany were all smiles upon first sight. He rented a car and had made the drive to Philly to meet up with her, as she'd rented a room in downtown Center City at the Marriott Hotel. Their night was to be filled with affection, as they had plans to go out to dinner, then next, attend an event of formal setting at a social gathering near South Street, an art gala. Tiffany made all the arrangements and scheduling.

Montell showed up in some of the best attire he'd ever spent good money for. Dude was dressed in a pair of Tom Ford slacks, black in color, a matching button-down shirt which had French cuffs at the wrist, catchy links to pin them together, and a vest to accent the look. The belt he had on matched the butter soft Wingtip Italian shoes he styled and profiled in. His diamond studded earrings were identical to the cuff links, as they were a twin set. And of course, Montell had on a sporty timepiece— a watch Mandy had bought for him on his birthday— a large dial rectangular Cartier which cost $5,000. He sought to really impress her with his appearance.

Tiffany had on a dark blue colored pants suit with a pair of metallic blue flats by Prada, gold hoop earrings, and her hair nicely done. Montell tapped on the hotel room door, room 227. She opened without asking who it was, as he'd texted on the ride up on the elevator. They both stared in silence at one another with smiles on their faces and shiny eyed. He stepped through the door entrance to greet her with a hug. Montell then kissed her on the forehead.

"Hello Tiffany. How are you?" he asked.

"I'm well, Montell. And yourself?" Tiffany responded.

"I'm well now. Thank God," he gave the glory to the Most High, as he had the words of his mother in mind in his response.

"No matter what you do son or how terrible things may get for you, always keep the Lord in mind and never forget him on no accord."

Tiffany looked into Montell's light brown eyes with those green cat eyes of hers and continued to smile.

"I hate the fact you had to go through all of those terrible channels with Verena and through life with those legal ordeals, Montell," she stated. "You're simply too good of a person to have to suffer as you have," Tiffany added.

"Well, I'm definitely in the hopes things will be good from this point forward. But the upside to it is, I still have you as a friend, Tiffany. And I'm thankful for that," Montell replied.

"If only you knew how good I feel just to have this opportunity to see your face physically again, and to also be able to enjoy some time out with you," she remarked.

"Likewise, Tiff. Likewise. So, what did you have in mind for us to get into tonight?" Montell wanted to know.

"Well, of course dinner, and I'd like to go to an art gala, and jazz show I heard about on the radio station here in the Tri-state area, WJJZ one oh six point one," she said to him.

"Oh. Dinner, an art gala, and a jazz event. It sounds like we getting classy tonight," he remarked and smiled while rubbing his hands together to further express his excitement. Tiffany returned a smile of her own and they were out.

***

They returned roughly five hours later to the hotel. While situated in the room, comfortable, and sipping on a bottle of Champagne, Moët, their conversation was mostly about the time Montell was housed in the prison Tiffany formerly worked, Phillips State Prison, and on the brief but pleasant affair which he had with her friend Verena. Tiffany related to Montell many other personal revelations which she'd been told by Verena herself on how things was between the warden and the inmate. Montell still couldn't believe the fact Verena had put anyone in her business. And at the same time, it was her best friend, a female, who was more like the sister she never had than anything. So, he had no problem from that point in knowing no one else knew. It could spell trouble with the law.

The talk between the two took a turn towards intimacy, and lead to a level of foreplay, then on to deeper things.

Montell was finally able to know what Tiffany's sex game was hitting for.

By the end of the night, he was able to relieve his mind from the many difficulties he'd faced in his life with a strong round of protected sex with Tiffany. They lay and continued to pillow talk until the crack of dawn and the sun fully rising. She enjoyed him and he enjoyed her. They both felt the wait was worth it.

Chapter 19

Tamron arrived in the capital city of Colombia, Bogota. Pete had his workers go to the airport to pick her up from there, as he was in Medellin, a city in the northwest part of where she'd arrived. A hotel suite had been reserved and Tamron rested on the first night in the South American Country.

The next day, she'd been driven to the second home of Pete to meet up with him, finally. He was happy to lay eyes on this bold, Spanish speaking black female hustler from the United States, who was looking to continue in playing on the dangerous field of the drug trade. Likewise, Tamron was pleased herself to be in total control of her new-found career as being a dealer, and at experiencing the type of start she was "blessed" to have by meeting with the plug directly, on his turf, and speaking his language.

"Greetings, Señorita Tamron," Pete said in his native language, Spanish.

"Hello Pete," How are you sir. Tamron replied with a smile and an extended hand. They got the formalities over and done with, then took a seat at the dining table in the mansion, as Pete had his servant pour them cocktails to drink.

Aside Pete, was his sister, Lydia, and a female associate, one who Tamron was already familiar with, Benita, the wife of Angel. Pete ordered her to be there prior to Tamron, to be sort of a reliable voice to co-sign the work Tamron has already put in, and on the supervision of the money, along with the progress of Tamron's growth in relations to Pete's organization.

"This here is, Lydia, Miss Tamron," Pete said to introduce the two, as they both shook the hand of each other. "And of course, you are in the know of who she is," he referred to Benita," Tamron Smiled and then shook Benita's hand as she smiled while remaining silent as Pete communicated the plan and his orders.

"So, Miss Tamron, this companion of yours, Montell, he's gotten himself into some really big trouble with the authorities I've come to learn," Pete stated.

"Yes Señor, that's correct. And I have nothing whatsoever to do with that guy any longer. He's dead to me," Tamron responded and expressed.

"Good. Good. Because the problems he's gotten himself in shall only warrant death to fall upon him," Pete vented.

Tamron continued to look at him in silence as he brainstormed and thought of a game plan to keep the movement going through her of his narcotic supply.

The day was a Friday and Tamron wasn't due to return to the states until the Monday to come. Pete desired to link Lydia up with Tamron and Benita in forging an acquaintance between the three in his cause. He wanted Tamron to become familiar with Lydia, as, when the time was to be at hand for her, Tamron, to begin being supplied directly by Pete with Montell completely removed out the picture, then Lydia would be the supervisor of operation in totality, and Tamron would be obligated to report to her and her only.

There would be no further need to simply report to Angel and Benita to pick up product and drop off cash. It would be Lydia's position at the point of new management.

"Miss Tamron," Pete spoke again. "My only duty today was to introduce the both of you to my brilliant assistant I have her in Miss Lydia," Pete added and gestured with his open hand in the direction of her.

"It's my pleasure Pete to be here in this beautiful country, and to also meet, Miss Lydia," Tamron said with a smile.

"Wonderful. It is my plan to have the three of you conduct and handle business in my name once you're to return. I will save the details of all there is to be for Sunday, when we are to finalize the deal. But until then, I would like for you lovely ladies to have the opportunity to enjoy all the luxuries and pleasures Colombia and myself have to offer," Pete lastly stated and bowed his head to wish them well before exiting the dining room.

Lydia and her personal assistant had orders to take Tamron and Benita out and about to restaurants, social events, and other places of interest for the duration of their stay, basically to keep them company and entertained until Sunday when the final phase of the visit was to occur.

Chapter 20

The Sunday arrived and they were all back at the table brokering a deal.

"So, Miss Tamron, before I am to agree to anything, I would like to know the setup of the organization which you lead?" Pete inquired.

Tamron then spoke up to explain her position as this turned out to be the opportunity she'd long awaited and the fulfillment of her Uncle Leroy's words when he mentioned to her "all you've got to do is prove to him you can handle all he supply you with, and have him paid on time, that's it TeeTee."

"Yes Pete, please allow me to relate all you ask of. Me and my people are very effective in selling product, as I've already proven. And we made sure you got all of your money on time without a penny short, correct?" Tamron stated and then asked in a short simple and sweet fashion.

The wisdom of Uncle Leroy came to mind yet again," always remember TeeTee, the less said is the best said. Less is more. Never give him more than what he ask of you. And in this case, the only thing needed to be known is you can move product and you will have all the money paid on time like agreed upon."

Pete smiled at the wits and fast thinking of Tamron, as she'd impressed him and convinced all at the same time.

"Yes, Yes Miss Tamron, you are correct," Pete responded. "However—"

"Well, that's all which truly matters, Pete," she cut in and capped, leaned back in her chair and took a sip of the expensive wine from the most exquisite glass the world over, courtesy of Pete.

"Miss Tamron, I ask of you to please, from this point, allow me to speak and not be interrupted, as these are crucial points I'm about to make, and I don't want for you to miss anything, as this is serious business," Pete expressed as he gauged the energy Tamron gave off, construed his face to an angry stare, and allowed his demeanor to take on that of a man who wish not to be over talked by a woman.

Tamron then humbled herself and took heed of the fact she was far away from home in another country on the turf of a notorious drug lord and seated at the table with him in one of his houses which was heavily guarded by armed killers who murdered at the crack of the whip by their leader, Pete.

She sat back in her seat and continued to slowly sip on the wine she had and listened attentive to everything Pete had to say about how he would do business.

"Miss Tamron, are you aware there is no way for you to turn back from this point? Are you knowledgeable of the lifestyle which you have now chosen to embrace?" Pete asked of her so as to have details she's understanding to what degree of trouble she could find herself in if anything goes wrong.

"I'm aware Señor. I have been taught and trained by one of the best, and he's groomed me for the moment that is now a reality," Tamron responded with confidence.

"So, I take it as you've been prepared by someone other than you ex-boyfriend, Montell?" Pete asked of her.

"That's correct too, Pete. It's absolutely correct. The person I speak of has a team of people himself, and we all get rid of the supply. So, there is no need to worry about your money coming up short or you not being paid. I don't want to have to pay you with my life, Señor," she expressed.

Pete grinned at the remark which she made and knew without a doubt, she was aware of the consequences if she fucked up.

"I'm glad to know you completely understand the formality of how things are to go once you've reached a certain level ... the severity of it all if you will," Pete stated.

"What's understood need not be explained, Señor," Tamron capped in reply.

"I like your level of confidence and sense of awareness, Tamron. I am to believe the business we are now about to get into will be prosperous. So, with that having been said, let's proceed, shall we," Pete said, then leaned over onto the glass table with his arms stretched out and rubbing his hands together.

"Miss Tamron, here is exactly how this business between us is to now go, okay. My plan is to supply you with one hundred kilos of pure top-quality Meth. Equally, one hundred kilos of Molly, the best party drug there is out there at the present moment; and possibly, two million pills of many types. You will owe me between four million and six million dollars, Miss Tamron. Can you handle such large amount of my product?" Pete wanted to know.

"That's not an issue for me and my people, Señor. Not an issue at all. Me and my people are qualified and capable to take on the task we have accepted to do," Tamron respond in a matter of fact type of way to the cartel leader without flinching.

"Are you sure, Miss Tamron, because I would like for all of my operations to continue to function properly without the slightest form of problems," Pete asked once more for complete assurance from Tamron.

"Señor, I'm positive. We're good, okay. I know fully my life is on the line if anything goes wrong, and no amount of excuses would work. Things have to go correct. They simply have to," she responded.

"Okay. Enough has been said on the agreement. When you are to return to the States, my assistant here, Lydia, is to be your new-found friend from here on out. She is to go where you go. She is to sleep where you are to sleep. She is to eat where you eat. And she is directly by your side at any time you are to have supply of mine. When not supplied, no Lydia. Am I clear on this?" Pete dictated and sought to know if or not his orders were understood.

"We're clear on this Señor Pete," she replied.

"Great. Now, on to other parts of this agreement," Pete said then gestured with his hand for Tamron and Lydia to shake each others so as to have agreement between the two. They did as he directed, and the meeting continued.

"Now, Miss Tamron, the format will remain the same on the pick-ups of the product with my associates, Angel and Benita, except, they will relocate to another farmhouse, due to your ex-boyfriend, Montell, having the knowledge of who they are, what they do, and where they live. With all the problems he's gotten himself into, there is absolutely no telling what he's subject to do or knows what information he may provide to the authorities at the point of him being finally arrested. Señor Angel is currently in the process of moving as we speak," Pete had stated.

"I'm understanding Pete. I'm glad to know we are already ahead and moving along well."

"That's the way I like to hear you comply. However, the real issue is this. How are we able to get a hand on Montell to eliminate the potential threat he now posed?" dsked Pete. "Is it a possibility you may be able to get a hand on this guy? Or do you have Someone else who may?" Tamron was asked, as he only sought straight answers.

"I believe eventually, Montell will get what is to come his way. It's only a matter of time Señor. A matter of time," replied Tamron.

"You are aware I have good reason to ask, correct? The guy knows entirely too much for me to remain comfortable in the fact he's still alive and able to live long enough to see another day. I want him done and out the way, completely," Pete expressed. He then paused to await the reply of Tamron which had to be well thought out long before she was to respond.

Chapter 21

Tamron thought long and deep before opening her mouth again. She didn't want to give Pete the wrong impression as if to suggest her and Montell was still connected some type of way, a far cry from the truth. She finally offered a response to Pete.

"I can assure you this much, Señor, I and my people will put forth our strongest effort to silence Montell and provide you the sense of comfort you desire once more by knowing he's done ... dead ... gone ... ain't no returning! All I ask is, for the business relations between you and I, to remain solidified," stated Tamron.

"Indeed, Miss Tamron, this is to be the business. Not a problem. All is left to complete this arrangement is for you to now immediately turn over your driver's license, your passport, and I'm gonna need a swab for DNA purpose," demanded Pete.

Tamron jarred her head at Pete's strange request. She furrowed her eyebrows and paused to determine if or not Pete was serious. He was.

"I must ensure you are who you say you are, Miss Tamron, and I must know how to contact and reach you in my time of need in the future," Pete said.

"It's no problem, Señor. I understand. I guess I don't have a choice at this particular point, do I," Tamron responded then eased her hand down into the Gucci tote bag where she kept her documents to retrieve the requested material.

Pete clapped his hands twice and in walked a male assistant of his wearing examination gloves and carrying a swab kit. The assistant also had on a white lab coat. Tamron was already familiar with the process and opened her mouth wide at the point of the assistant reaching her. The assistant thoroughly swabbed Tamron, then put the kit away. He then had taken hold of the documents which she had and was off to go make front and back copies. He also took pictures of the material and uploaded into an email account. Five minutes later, he returned everything to Tamron, as the talk between she and Pete continued.

Pete was sure to lay down all of the rules for Tamron to follow without fail, made mention of the logistics on how the narcotic supply would reach her, and on all he expected. She had direct instructions to follow those orders, as she knew Pete wouldn't accept anything less from her. She would become his new and special sales person of his product in her city of the States. Things held the potential to go really well for her, as she desired to be the superior boss bitch that the city of Atlanta has never been home to. The only issue which Tamron developed a problem with was, in the fact of Pete ordering Lydia to be the shadow of her. But Tamron felt overtime, once the business begun to prosper and produce the type of results Pete intended, he'd eventually relieve Lydia of her duties and have her to fall back and allow Tamron to continue in doing all she was to do. Also, Tamron had to be absolutely sure to conceale the fact of her uncle being part of law enforcement. Of all people, he was her most valuable asset and business partner.

The agreement between Pete and Tamron was sealed and the three-day meeting came to an end the Sunday night of. She'd been escorted back to her hotel suite which she was now to share with Lydia for they to rest up and ready themselves for the flight back to the states.

While relaxing and feeling good about how everything went, she pulled out her phone and contacted her Uncle Leroy to update him on the progress.

"Hello!" he answered.

"Hey Uncle Leroy. It's me, TeeTee," she responded in a low tone to keep Lydia out of her conversation.

"I'm aware, baby girl. Talk to me. Tell me something good will you," he stated.

"Tell you something good, huh. It's all good, Uncle Leroy. Everything went very smoothly. We're on our way to the top," she said ecstatically.

"Oh, we are huh? That's great. So, you did everything I told you to huh?" he's asked.

"To the letter," she replied.

"That's my niece. That's my dear niece there, I tell you. Now all left for us to do is to stay in it to win it, and all else will continue to fall in place. We can talk more once you get home, okay," the uncle lastly stated before they concluded the call.

Leroy's long-awaited opportunity to be able to expand the enterprise he'd worked so hard to build on the inside—he and his coalition of dirty cops—was upon him. He could hardly wait to begin moving the drug supply his brothers daughter coincidentally stumbled upon a connection to. All was left was for him to watch the throne. That was it, watch the throne.

Chapter 22

Jamie returned to Atlanta from his brief visit to his hometown of Jacksonville. He had it in mind to proceed on about the business of the club and find a way to disassociate himself and the business from Montell, being Montell had more problems on his hands to deal with than he and the others was able to handle. The more and more Jamie thought on things, the more he'd came to realize, Geno had a point and made a lot of sense with all he'd mentioned about Montell, about him being bad news, and he would be the one to cause their downfall the second time around if they were ever to find themselves in trouble again with the law.

Jamie, being the most civil-minded and the least with problems of the three which remained, had a decision to make on the involvement of his friends on their part of the club. Roderick was someone who was forced to inherit a street team and drug organization which his brother left behind, which requires the majority of his attention and time over the club. And Montell, well, it's already known of the drama which he's now facing and eventually would have to deal with at some point.

Prior to Jamie pulling the trigger in making the call on what to do about the initial deposit of Montell and Roderick, he felt the need to have a conversation with the other business partners who had an interest in Seduction City, Felix and Geno, and of course, the nephew represents both.

They were at the Club together when this particular talk was to take place.

"Geno, what's good bruh?"

"Check this out right. I've thought over a lot of things, and I've come to the conclusion, you've been right in many ways," Jamie begun.

"I had been wondering what was taking you so long to see what was obvious my nigga. I've been in this shit too long, Jamie, not to know exactly how it goes. But go ahead, I'm listening," Geno responded.

"Yeah, so, what my plan to do is, I'm gonna pay back the money Montell and Roderick put in to be part of the ownership. I'm gonna give them their money and let them be on their way. Rod don't seem to be around or interested anymore, and Montell, we already know what's going on with him. So, once I take care of them, it'll simple be you and me, the ones who are present and own the club," Jamie informed.

"And when is this supposed to take place?" asked Geno.

"It'll be soon. It'll be real soon, my nigga. Just know it'll be taken care of and all the heat we've been feeling here from the GBI and the local police behind the bullshit Mo got going on, should come to an end from there," Jamie said.

"I like the sound of all that Jamie. I really do. I'm glad to know you see the bigger picture, big dawg. Just stay real with me, and I'll stay real with you," Geno proposed and extended his arm to shake Jamie's. They locked in on the agreement, and a new chapter had begun for they and Seduction City, as the two remaining owners, Jamie and Geno, finally agreed on something worthy.

Chapter 23

Verena progressed in her recovery from the light coma she'd been in following the overdose and was transferred from the hospital to the psych-ward in the northeast part of the state. The judicial authority who had been assigned the case ordered she remain in the institution on an indefinite basis until she'd been deemed to no longer be of a danger to herself or anyone else. She wasn't allowed a visit from anyone for a minimum of thirty days upon her intake process, as she was forced to go through a series of tests and examinations for placement purposes.

The state officials also pumped Verena with all types of medication and injection shots to keep her sedated. Verena had a difficult time coming to terms with the predicament she'd put herself in by attempting to take her own life. Her mind had been greatly altered in many ways from the point of her being very near non-responsive and oxygen depleted from entry into her system. But she managed to recover to a point of near normalcy. Her mental faculties returned, and throughout her examinations, she'd been put through a repeated questioning process with the top mental health specialist at the facility.

The doctor asked," Ma'am, are you Verena Evette Gordon? Is this your name?"

"Yes. That's my name," she replied in a very low and hissing tone of voice.

"Okay, do you know where you are, ma'am?" the male doctor asked of Verena.

"I believe I do. What happen, and why am I here?" Verena wanted to know.

Upon entry of the ward, she wasn't mentally competent to be put through the series of questions now asked of her. The officials had to wait until she was able to follow through.

"So, you don't know why you're here? Do you have any knowledge of what happened to you?" The questions continued.

"My babies. Where are my kids?" she asked and begun to look around frantically in the hopes she'd locate her twins. The sedation had worn thin. "My babies. Where are they?" she asked again.

The doctor leaned down and begun to write in his notepad. He lifted his head again and looked at Verena to continue with the questions.

"So do you or don't you know where you are now located?" he questioned further through the glass barrier that existed between he and Verena, as she continued to look around frantically inside the cubicle where she sat, apparently oblivious to it all upon no longer being drugged up.

Verena sat both hands on her knees and begun to tap the heels of her feet on the floor, as she had on a pair of loud orange flip-flops without socks. She put her hands on her head and slightly gripped her hair, then ran her hands through before placing them back on her knees.

"Miss Gordon, if you're not aware of where you are or what happened, I'll tell you. You attempted to harm yourself and had to be placed into a better situation to prevent such, and to also get you some help, okay," the doctor spoke up again.

"I did what?" Verena questioned, as she had lost all memory of what actually took place. The oxygen shortage to her brain caused this. "Are my babies okay?" she wanted to know.

"Yes, Miss Gordon. Your kids are fine," he replied.

"Wooo! Thank God," she exhaled and let out in relief.

"Miss Gordon, I would like to know, why did you attempt to harm yourself? What pushed you to the point?" The medical personnel wanted to know and sat at the ready to document everything which was to exit her mouth.

Verena had a dazed and disorientated look about her face and appeared downcast with emotion behind the question.

"Miss Gordon, what was it that pushed you to want to harm yourself might I ask?" The doctor repeated.

Verena protruded her lips, paused momentarily, and then provided an answer. "He left me. My kids father left me for another woman. How could he do me like that? How could he? We were supposed to be in love. We were supposed to be so committed and dedicated to one another. Then he turned and left me and our babies to go be with another woman. No!" Verena slammed a fist down hard on the counter of the cubicle where she sat.

"So, you say your kids father left you, Verena? Is this the reason why you tried to harm yourself?" The doctor asked back-to-back questions. Verena simply said nothing and stared off into space continuously. The psychiatrist wrote down the exact words and demeanor of Verena as he was in the process of play-writing a script for her to act out on the stage and he was the great William Shakespeare himself.

All of a sudden, Verena had gotten quiet as kept and sat motionless as ever. She began to cry and the doctor took it as his cue to end the questions and the examination for the day. The handlers took hold of and escorted her back to the cell where they kept her safely secured, in a space which had padded walls and discarded Styrofoam plates that she'd half eaten and tossed to the side. Her medication dosage was increased by the doctor the same day.

Chapter 24

Eric and Joleena were making great progress in their relationship. They had gotten to where they lived together in the home Eric had purchased through bank approval from the account he and Verena opened together. Joleena no longer shared a house with her cousin, as she had before becoming involved with the guy who fathered twins and had left her to be more focused on all the two of them had established.

Joleena enjoyed the idea of having Eric all to herself without any interference from no other woman, especially that arrogant and spiteful bitch, Verena. But opposite of what she thought of Verena as a person, she sided with her in regard to feelings and as a woman.

Joleena didn't like the way Eric lied to her and held back the fact of having kids. She also didn't agree on any level how he had abandoned Verena and the twins to be with her. Hell, if he has kids by her and dumped the mother of his two children to be with me, he'd do the same to me with another woman, Joleena long thought to herself once being made aware.

She never expressed those feelings nor attempted to communicate them to Eric. She simply did what most women would do as it applies to a man they loved; she kept them to herself until there was to be a point she could utilize an angle to gain an advantage.

One day, they had a conversation, and the topic was around her and Eric getting custody of his kids until Verena was mentally stable to do her part. This was not too long after Verena was checked into the psych ward, or as Eric put it, she was checked into the "crazy house"

"Eric, what's the situation with your kid's mother. And if anybody, who has the kids?" Joleena asked of him, as they sat on the couch in the living room of their house and watched TV shows.

"To tell you the truth, Joleena, I dont know the situation of that crazy bitch, and frankly don't give a fuck! Her silly-ass shouldn't had tried to kill herself. That's all on her. But from what I know about my kids, they're in good hands, I'm sure. Verena, has a best friend named Tiffany who's the godmother of our kids, and more than likely, she's the one who has them," Eric said.

"But I'm curious to know, Eric, why are you not trying to gain custody of your own children, that way we can both take care of them until their mother is well?" Joleena pressed.

"Joleena, when the time is right for us to have our kids in our custody and away from their crazy mother, then we'll have them, but until then, I for one, really don't have the time nor the patience to be running behind and watching kids. I'm busy trying to get things situated and in place out there in the world to take care you and I, and once that's done, then and only then, will I be ready to include others into the picture," Eric stated and gestured with his finger towards the outside as he explained his position to Joleena.

"Eric, listen to yourself for a moment will you. Now how do you think all of what you just said sound to me?" Joleena vented with a question.

"I don't know. How did it sound to you?" he replied, now facing Joleena as they locked eyes in such an intense moment.

"How do it sound to me? How do it sound to me?" she repeated. "Eric, are you being serious right now!" she fired back.

"And why wouldn't I be?" he shot in a sarcastic manner.

"Do you really want to go there? Would you really like for me to tell you exactly how that shit sounds to me?" Joleena responded to the challenged.

"Feel free to go right on ahead," he urged with his sarcasm.

Joleena paused before speaking any further as she stared at Eric as if to say, I don't believe this motherfucker. Then she went on. "Eric, how that shit sounds to me is like, you don't have a care nor concern for your own kids, dude. You make me afraid to think if I was to someday have your kids, that you may do me the same as you've done to her," Joleena expressed.

"Joleena, you don't know the half of it, okay. If you really knew Verena enough, you'd know my reason for leaving her was based on the fucked-up attitude she has, and on how unhappy I was being in a relationship with her. None of it, or this for that matter, has anything to do with the kids. Besides, Verena has enough of my money and of her own money to cover any expenses that are to come along with Tiffany keeping our kids until things are right," Eric had explained.

"And how are you so sure of that Eric? Money don't fix everything."

"It's because I know Verena, and you don't. Besides, stop concerning yourself with the business of other people. Don't be so quick to try and be in the middle of a dispute between me and my ex, okay," he'd stated in a serious tone.

"News flash, Eric. I *am* in the middle! And I *am* the reason! It's my responsibility to help you make things right between you and her, so that things could be right between you and I," Joleena spat then paused to await a response from Eric. He said nothing.

"Now get that through your head, will you," she lastly stated, then got up to go and finish preparing the taco meal they were to eat for dinner and would afterwards wash down with a nice bottle of wine.

Joleena definitely felt some type of way about the ill-treatment and fucked up attitude which Eric displayed towards the mother of his kids, and at the neglect of the kids all together. She never truly expressed those concerns and had felt better to keep them to herself until a time was to come, as it almost always do, to communicate them to him, and by then, if it won't be too late for Eric to hit the reset button and start over.

Joleena did manage to warn Eric of the troubles he was beginning to create for himself at the point of her initiating an argument with him concerning his ex and their kids. Issues she had nothing to do with. But he paid no attention nor took any heed. He was beginning to expose himself in many regards, and Joleena didn't appreciate the ugly character which he'd concealed from her for far too long.

Likewise, on the opposite end of, Eric knew exactly how low down and grimy Verena could get or have been towards him and Montell, and he felt the need to get back at her behind the things she'd done in the starting phase of their relationship. He felt if Verena would do Montell like she had to be with him, she'd do him that way to be with someone else.

And on the flip side of this, it was no different than how Joleena felt. So, the untrustworthy cycle would continue to revolve without someone attempting to break it, concluding that love and loyalty wouldn't be properly established.

Chapter 25

The commissioner of the Georgia Department of Corrections was contacted by the IRS behind some information which they'd received from a former Warden in the state. The former Warden, Verena Evette Gordon, reported to them several names and personal information of inmates which had been utilized fraudulently on income tax claims, and funds were returned on the majority of those filings north of $2,000,000.

The IRS made the commissioner totally aware of all the intel which one—Gordon—had provided. In addition to the names and identity of those she had direct knowledge as to who was the perpetrators of the schemes that had been worked from the confines and restraints of the inside, Gordon gave up dates, and reported how the claims were prepared and filed, both electronically and by way of paper submission. Her information was very detailed and accurate, as if she'd personally perfected the scams herself.

The DOC had confirmed indeed, Gordon worked as a Warden for a time being, and the names of the people which she had memory of whose information was used, did in fact reside at the prison around the time made known of the scam being worked by four persons whose names she also provided— Montell, Eric, Jamie, and Roderick.

All the Doc had to do from that point was to have the IRS to run the names of all inmates who resided at Phillips State Prison during the time Gordon was the Warden, and they shall find indeed, the inmates names which showed as having filed for income tax was locked up, and it was absolutely impossible for them to have been employed to have returns claimed. The IRS had already performed their investigations to corroborate what Gordon reported, and what the Georgia DOC assisted them on. The IRS then wanted to personally interview Gordon on everything she'd reported on the phone. The IRS had a little surprise for her kept under their sleeve which was to be revealed either during the interview or soon thereafter. They were on it.

Chapter 26

In Atlanta, Geno and Felix had a conversation related to all he and Jamie discussed concerning *X-ing* out Montell and Roderick from ownership over SC. "Nephew, I'm so glad you stepped to Jamie and brought it to his attention it wouldn't be nothing but a problem and even a disaster if we was to continue on with that hot-ass friend of his, Montell, and the other one who didn't really want shit to do with the club anyway, to continue being lied to us on this business. This is definitely the best thing for us to do, cut them negros off," Felix said to Geno.

"Hey unc, I made your boy Jamie an offer he couldn't refuse. It was either get rid of them niggaz and roll with my plan, or I was gonna do away with all of the together, you smell me," Geno capped in reply.

"Shit, you know me nephew, I don't give a damn about anything, so long as I get my cut when the time is to be paid. And besides, I know you gonna take care of my interest, because that's also your interest too. That's exactly why I made it my business to bring you on board, so you can see to things the way we want it to go anytime a situation occurs, as we have now," Felix complimented and acknowledged.

"Ha ha ha ha ha! I like how you put that unc," Geno remarked.

"You know what it is nephew, it's family first ain't it."

"And you got to know that unc. If it wasn't for you, then we already know none of this SC shit would have been possible. Them niggaz thought they were too slick for their own fucking good, unc. But not when it comes to us thinking ahead of things. Besides, ain't none of them niggaz from Atlanta anyway! They ain't got no business being over us in our own city no-how. What the fuck was they thinking! Like we wouldn't eventually recognize that shit," stateed Geno.

"Damn nephew. I never gave it any thought. Now that you mentioned it, it ain't none of the boys from around here," Felix responded.

"Trust me unc. I know. I was only waiting for the right opportunity to bring it to your attention, right before we were to take action and get them the fuck out of our way, like now. But Jamie, he cool. I like ol' Jamie. He's open-minded and capable of seeing shit in the right way to give him a better angle to negotiate and be able to live to see another day. That's the only reason I ain't made a move to get him out the way. He's about business and don't want no smoke," Geno said to his uncle on the assessment of Jamie.

"So now all is left is for us to sit tight and see what type of reaction is to come from that Montell cat and the other one, Rod," Felix said.

"Unc. Listen to yourself for a moment, will you," Geno stated.

"What nephew?" responded Felix.

"Are you serious, nigga! Now be honest with me for a moment, will you. What type of reaction do you possibly think Montell is gonna have behind us bopping his ass out of the way? Need I remind you, that nigga on the run from the police, for raping and killing a fucking white bitch! We probably doing him a favor by giving him the money back than anything. I'm sure he can use it. And the boy Rod, word has it, he's too busy trying to keep the game alive with his family up in Philly on everything his brother left behind. They need him more there than we do here. That's why he seem to be more away than present. Basically, what I'm trying to tell you is this, unc ... *fuck them niggaz!* And the only one I see has some sense out of them is Jamie, and if I wasn't able to get through to him in the time I did, I would've been busy thinking of a way to move his ass too! But he got smart, fast," Geno expressed, then got quiet as kept and awaited the response of his uncle. He simply looked at his nephew with a smirk about his face and didn't utter a word. Geno took his uncle's silence to be his acceptance of the underhanded plays he maintained in mind, but all along, Felix was aware he needed to keep close watch on Geno and not reveal too much. Least Geno may attempt to 'bop' him out the way too, as he put it.

"Unc listen," Geno continued," you say you want me to be your eyes, ears and face over here, right? That you need me to run things for you. Okay. This, I'm doing. All you got to do is continue to chill and let me do what I do," Geno urged.

"You have my approval on that nephew. Just please, whatever you do, don't get messy and do try to get too aggressive and do too much here," Felix stated and pointed to the floor indicating there at the clubs.

"No need to worry unc. Me and Razor got everything under our control. You, me, and the people on our team," Geno stated emphatically.

"That's good to know nephew. Let's continue to keep it that way, shall we,"

The conversation came to an end and Felix left them to be who they'd become, the right people he needed in place to push the agenda which he had in mind all along; money pouring in from multiple ways in the things he loved most ... women, social spots, and alcohol.

Felix had ambition to someday be the "Godfather" of the Atlanta night life, and at all cost, he was destine to see to it his dream to be such was to become a reality, long before his dying day approached. He'd patiently awaited for such opportunity, and at long last, the moments were at hand. Now all was left was for him to keep the greedy nature of his nephew under control for as long as he could, before Geno was to get the idea he'd become too big to listen to him anymore. Felix had a task to deal with. It was called," taming the beast of nephew."

Chapter 27

When Tragedy Strikes...

RODERICK and Montell were out and about, cruising through the city of Philly in one of the many luxury rides that the brother of his A-One once owned. It was the black cherry colored Mercedes Benz S550. This probably was A-One's most beloved vehicle when he was alive.

With Montell being a wanted man for the type of crimes he was accused of, one would think that his choice of vehicles to move around in, would be something more low key and discreet. But he'd developed a sense of comfort with the fake ID cards he now had, and he dressed in a more casual way, with designer clothing he now favored.

Roderick had no troubles with the law. And the car he drove was legit by all means. It hadn't been driven in months, and he made sure to take it to a Benz dealership for a tune-up the day he began driving it, so to putting miles on it how he saw fit. And so, he'd taken a liking to this luxury sedan.

The car was also one Khalib and a few of his people were all too familiar with, as the beef between the two families had escalated to new levels, with Roderick pulling the trigger himself, taking the life of one of Khalib's uncle. A bold move.

And now, one of Khalib's brothers—Yusuf—who knew too that the Benz belonged to the enemy. He knew of Roderick in a way and spotted him pushing the big-body automobile through the Bad Lands of North Philly. He begun to trail him, without Roderick ever taking notice of the potential danger that loomed.

"Yo Khal," the brother spoke over the phone once reaching out to Khalilb with information he wanted to tell him.

"What's good, bro."

"Yo. You not gonna believe this shit right here, bro."

"What's up?"

"How 'bout, I'm following behind the nigga A-One's brother, right now! He driving that Benz that his ass used to ride around in."

"Say word!" Khalib couldn't believe his ears.

"Word bro!"

"How you sure it 's him? And wait a minute. Which brother?" Dude wanted to be sure.

"The nigga, Rod. The one that had been away down south somewhere for all that time," he stated, making his brother totally aware.

"That's the nigga who killed unc, bro!" Khalib muttered. "Yo, who with you right now?"

"It's me and the fam. I got Womie with me."

"Yo Yu, I know I ain't even gotta tell y'all niggaz how to handle that shit, do I? And how do you know it's him exactly? The nigga Rod?"

"Because I seen the nigga's face when he got out the car to run in the store. He came out eating a hoagie, a cheese steak, or something like that," Yusuf responded with confirmation.

"So, is he by himself?"

"Nah. He got some other nigga with him."

"Shit, what the fuck. He can get it too, Yu! We got to act now and not let that bitch-ass nigga get away! Yo, y'all fire them pussies up, right now, and then, be ready to leave town when y'all done. No matter what, we gotta touch them niggaz now while the opportunity is at hand!"

Khalib gave the order for a hit. He ended the call on that note and wasn't expecting for his brother to call back until well after the fact of carrying out the mission at hand. They had to clap back at those who let off shots at them first. It was an eye for an eye and a tooth for a tooth.

***

YUSEF CONTINUED TO trail Roderick as he drove through the Bad Lands and taking in the scenes of the activity of the night life. He felt the urgency to act fast before Roderick took notice that someone was riding his bumper and actually do something to stop it.

The cousin, Wompie, now spoke up. "Say, Yu, what Khal want us to do?" he asked.

"Shit, you should already know the answer to that my nigga! We gotta light them niggaz up, cuz!" he stated.

Wompie immediately pulled out his pistol, cocked it, and situated a bullet in the chamber. Yusuf had done the same.

Nightfall was fully set in and the cover of darkness could conceal the actions that was in process of going down.

Roderick was driving down Allegheny Ave heading west towards Broad Street. When he got to the intersection of Allegheny and Glenwood, and in the process of turning off onto Glenwood to continue down this street, this was the point when Yusuf made his move. He cut Roderick off from making his left turn, causing him to hit the brakes and stop on the dime. Yusuf and Wompie, both hopped out of the Nissan Altima he was driving with guns up and immediately begun blasting away at their two targets. By the time Roderick or Montell looked up to take notice of the ambush, they were in grave danger. It was too little, too late. The guns were blazing already.

Boom-Boom-Boom-Boom-Boom-Boom-Boom!
Pop-Pop-Pop-Pop!
Boom-Boom!

Pop-Pop-Pop... Pop!
Boom!
Roderick was only able to throw the car's gear into reverse and nothing more. He definitely was unable to hit the gas pedal and gun it going backwards before the first bullet struck him and rendered Roderick unconscious. Montell caught several bullets himself in the upper body and was too conscienceless. The Benz slowly rolled backwards, over the edge of the sidewalk, and finally came to a stop upon impact against a fire hydrant.

Yusuf and Wompie moved quickly and jumped back into the Nissan and sped away from the scene of the crime. The both of them—Roderick and Montell—were riddled with lead from the guns used against them, along with the S550, as they were slumped in the car and hurt pretty badly. A nearby neighbor of the area had called 9-1-1 to make a report, and the ambulance, along with Philly Police, would soon be there to investigate what had actually happened, and to rush them to the hospital.

Team Khalib had struck again and happened to tally up one on the ops in the process. He was pleased to know his people had done a very good job. Or did they?

***

Montell and Roderick were taken to the nearest hospital following the shooting attack. This happened to be Temple University Hospital which wasn't too far from the location of the incident. Although the two were riddled with bullets and in critical condition, they would survive. The only thing neither of them would enjoy fully again were their physical abilities. This would be lost forever.

Roderick was the one who got it the worst. One of the lead missiles pierced his neck and damaged the spine, resulting in him being paralyzed from the neck down. He was also hit by the assailant's gunfire in the left portion of

127

his torso and in the right hand. An insignificant graze wound came about on the left side of his head as well, but this was the least of his worries, in comparison to the other lethal infliction he suffered.

As with Montell, he was shot in the left side of his torso, resulting in a collapsed lung; another wound to the left shoulder; and another to his inner right thigh. He was lucky to get away with his life, in the aftermath of the brazen ambush.

Awakening from the second surgery he had to have performed days later, Montell was greeted by four law enforcement officials. There were two Pennsylvania State Troopers and two GBI personnel members. The lead investigator of the GBI, a Blake Gabber, initiated the formal arrest.

"Montell Jermaine McNeil. How you doing, buddy? I'm glad to know you're still with us and didn't walk towards the light, if you get what my drift," he stated. The officer then presented the shiny badge he was a possession of, placing the bright metal object so close to Montell's face, that the glare from it hurt his eyes. Montell had to turn his head away, to prevent any vision damage.

Still disoriented from the anesthesia medication administered to perform the surgery, Montell let out, "who are you? And what's going on?" Although really weakened and speaking with the slurred tongue, he was able to gain an understanding of what was taking place in real time.

The law enforcement official then said to him," well... being that you asked... I do have a duty to make you aware of your grim reality. I'm Georgia Bureau investigator Blake Gabbert, and this gentleman here," he turns and points, "is an an esteemed colleague of mine, Mr. Brad Moxley. And these two fine guys here," he turns again and pointed to the troopers holding post on both sides of the hospital room door, "are State patrolmen from Pennsylvania, since we're on their jurisdictional turf, to do what we're now doing."

Montell responded, "and what's that?"

"What's what, Mr. McNeal?"

"This what you're now doing?" Montell wheezed out and winced in pain by doing so.

"To be straightforward with you, Mr. McNeal, me and my colleague here, flew all the way from Georgia today, to formally arrest you on the outstanding warrant you've managed to elude us on for the past couple of months. And had it not been for you getting shot and a blood sample taken to prove your identity through a DNA database system, we probably would have still been trying to get a lead from someone on your whereabouts. So... without further delay, please allow me to get on with it," Gabbert out. He then proceeded. "Montell Jermaine McNeal, you are under arrest, for the rape and murder of one: Mandy Barfield. You have a right to remain silent. Anything you say can and will be used against you on a court of law. You have a right to an attorney. If you cannot afford one, the court will appoint one to represent you...." Investigator Gabbert was sure to properly and fully read Montell his Miranda rights. He didn't want to screw up anything, as far as the case was concerned. It could potentially cost him his career had he done so.

"So, I guess this is it for me, huh... the end of the road for a guy like me. How much worse could it be? I get shot and was nearly killed, then, while recovering in the hospital from my injuries, I get told that I'm under arrest for '*rape*'—*o*f all crimes—and '*murder,*' adding further insult to injury."

"Well, look at it this way, at least you do get to breathe and walk again, unlike your long-time buddy who's in the room next door in ICU as well. He only gets to breathe. He's gonna be paralyzed from the neck down for the rest of his life. Poor guy. But whoever those guys were that shot you two... they wanted you dead. However, the shooting itself, is not within our hands to investigate. And once me and my partner are done with our process, the Pennsylvania officials have a few questions for you, okay."

"Man, whatever, man. What the fuck ever!" Montell uttered, waving off the officer then turning his head away from him to stare in the opposite direction.

Montell's memory slowly made its way back to him, and at the direct observation of all the medical equipment that was connected to him, he'd come to the conclusion that he was fortunate enough to have survived the hit he'd gotten caught up in. The breathing tube supplying oxygen through his nostrils brought to mind the tinge of pain he experienced on the left side of the body.

Turning his head back towards the officer Montell asks, "how many times was I hit?" He really had no idea of how severe the situation was he lived survived to question about.

"Quite a few, is all I can tell you. One of your lungs is barely working, and you may not be able to fully use the left arm of yours again. But no need to worry, the Georgia Department of Corrections, is gonna be sure to take *good* care of you, once we're able to secure the conviction of you for the crimes we now have you in custody for," stated Gabbert.

"Man, why you gotta come at me with all that? Ain't you got any consideration for the wounded, or any compassion for the next man? I done been shot up. I could have died. My body is not gonna be whole again. And I'm totally aware now, that I'm gonna go from this hospital room to a jail cell, to await trial. So won't you give me a break?" Montell said.

"Well, if anything, all you just said is based on facts. I can't dispute that. But if you have something you wanna say to me, that may possibly help you out with the fight you're gonna be up against down in Georgia, that'll be fine, ya know," Gabbert stated.

"Yeah. I got something I wanna say. I ain't do it! And I want a lawyer present for each and every interview I'm subject to have with you people moving forward. Therefore, anything else from you or anybody else from law enforcement, must come to an end. How about that for kicks!"

"Suit yourself. But one final thing on that. You've got an extradition process to go through, once you're finally freed from the hospital here. My advice to you is to not fight it, because we know who you are, and we have the right person in custody."

"I know how this goes, man. Thanks anyway."

"My pleasure."

The verbal exchange between the two came to an end. The medication caused Montell to dose back to sleep. He was in the hope that maybe when he awaken again, that the raw reality he falsely perceived to only be a nightmare, would all be over with. How mistaken was he.

Chapter 28

The information about Montell's arrest in Philly reached Georgia in a hurry. Channel Five News station reported his capture, and all of Atlanta and the region was in the know of his current status. This included Montell's family and friends. Tamron received firsthand information from her police uncle, Leroy. He told her all about it the minute he got word.

"Hello, Uncle Leroy. How are you?" she answered her phone at the notice of his name flash across the screen. She did her best to disguise the immense degree of sorrow and emotional pain she experienced behind the brief mention of Montell being arrested, but Leroy was not fooled. He knew how in love his niece was with the guy and kept quiet about what he knew about her mood.

"Hey! I'm fine, TeeTee. Thanks for asking. I called because I don't know if or not you were aware, but that ex-boyfriend of yours, Montell McNeal—"

"I saw it on the news, Uncle Leroy. He was arrested in Philadelphia," Tamron cut him off to say.

"So I see you know already. That'll save me some time with explaining the details of everything. But here is what I don't need you to lose the understanding on... the business that we now got going on. He's *dead* to you, remember?"

In a low somber slow release of words, Tamron responded, "yes Uncle Leroy. I remember what we've went over already about him."

"That's good to know. And now all you gotta do is keep to that. So simple to do, right?"

"You're right. It is." At least this was what her mouth said to her uncle. But the love she still held so dear to in her heart and in her spirit for Montell, said something else altogether. "So, what all is it that he's being charged with? And will he be brought back to Georgia to have a trial? When will he be brought back, I meant to say?" she asked.

"For starters, we got his ass charged with *'rape'*... *'murder'*... drug possession, and possession of multiple firearms. But when the DA eventually indicts him, I'm more than sure that they're gonna hang more charges on his ass. The same way that I'm sure once the trial is at its end, the jury is gonna hang all *'guilty'* verdicts on his ass too! It ain't a doubt in my mind about that. It'll take an absolute miracle from God himself, for a jury to come back with *'Not Guilty'* verdicts against this nigga's ass, TeeTee! I swear, it will."

"They came back with *'Not Guilty'* verdicts on O.J., and he was accused of killing not one but *two* white people."

"Well now... this nigga Montell, ain't no O.J., now is he? And O.J. had money, and a *'Dream Team'* of nothing but the best lawyers that money could buy."

"They came back with *'Not Guilty'* verdicts on Casey Anthony. And the whole world had already convicted her in the court of public opinion long before her trial started."

"Look, TeeTee, okay. Let Uncle Leroy be very clear with you for a moment, if I may. And I'mma be brutally blunt with you on this too... because I don't wanna have to say it no more. You either with me and all the way in on what I stand for and what we got going on... or... you against me and the motion we having right now. So, which side you on? Because I gave you a fair warning from the get-go, that this shit was one way in and *NO* way out, so long as you are alive. Dead people can't reveal no secrets! Can't no dead motherfucker, snitch somebody out. And that's why I told you that... this nigga Montell... was *dead* to you, as he should be. But while you were down in Columbia, what all did Pete say to you on this?"

"Pete said that the only way we're gonna know that we're safe from being ratted on, is if Montell was no longer living."

"So, Pete wants him dead too?"

"Basically, yeah."

"*Humph!*" Leroy scoffed into the phone. "And to answer the other question you had about your *beloved* Montell... In the next couple of weeks, he'll be extradited back here to face justice. It would've happened sooner, had he and the other boy he was with, not gotten all shot up and shit. And you got your Uncle Leroy, all outta character and cussing like I'm crazy, having a conversation with you about a nigga who doesn't mean you any good... a goddamn *'dead man,'* he is!" Leroy stated emphatically. He had more to say. "And why you seem to be taking up for that dude anyway like you doing? That's what I wanna know, TeeTee. Because at the end of the day, you already done made your decision on what you wanted to do. You already done made your decision about the business that we currently got going on. Ain't no way out, TeeTee."

"I'm not tryna take up for Montell, Uncle Leroy. And I'm not tryna find a way out of the business obligations I now have. Honestly, I'm not. It's just that when you love somebody, you love somebody."

"TeeTee! What the fuck love gotta do with it?! Please tell me that?"

"Truthfully, Uncle Leroy, I don't believe that Montell did what he's being accused of. I don't. I'm sorry. I know that man better than that. And never in a million years will I believe that Montell actually raped and killed a woman, then be so stupid, to leave drugs and guns in the house only to be found, along with the body. I just don't believe that. And I'm being logical about it. I know him."

"Well... all that's up for a jury to decide on. And his problems with the law or otherwise, ain't your problems anymore. Because you already done took care of the half million dollar problem he left you stuck with, along with a little help from me. But TeeTee, I don't wanna continue on with having a full conversation with you about this guy, Montell. I just called to let you know that we got him, and to know what type of head space you would be in over the fact, because the show must go on. It's a must that it do. Big business is at stake here. And this comes before anything else. And on another note, Landy asked about you again too. We spoke earlier today. She says call her sometime," Leroy made the niece aware.

I actually will do this today. Besides, me and Landy definitely need to talk, like today we need to, now that you've mentioned it, Uncle Leroy, Tamron though over.

"I completely understand that we got major business to handle moving forward, Uncle Leroy. And I'mma be sure to call Landy sometime soon too. Thanks for seeing to it that I stay on point. And thanks for letting me know Landy asked about me," Tamron said, now looking to bring the call to an end.

An idea came to her throughout this instance. One she couldn't resist the temptation to pursue.

"You take care now, TeeTee, you hear. And Uncle Leroy loves you."

"You do the same, Uncle Leroy. And I love you too."

The call came to an end between the two.

***

Immediately, Tamron went into her contacts on her phone and drew up Leroy's daughter Landy's number. There was something urgent that the longtime girlfriend of a man charged with serious violent felonies, needed to converse with her lawyer cousin about. Especially so, with Landy and Montell, already having knowledge of one another, with Landy being in the North already (New York City) and with

Montell, still being held up North himself in a county jail, awaiting to be transported to Georgia.

Tamron knew that more than likely, Montell had no lawyer yet to represent him in the case. And with Landy stationed only ninety miles to the north of where Montell was, she could visit with him and help he and Tamron get ahead of things, weeks in advance before the extradition was initiated.

The time was right at 7:00 P.M. On a Wednesday. Tamron texted the cousin of hers first, to be sure she was available for a call.

HER: *Landy! Hey. It's me, TeeTee. I got a new number now. And I apologize for not getting it to you sooner. Uncle Leroy told me you asked about me and wanted me to call. Can you talk at the moment? I really need to speak with you.*

Nearly ten minutes passed from when Tamron sent out the text. Landy eventually replied.

Landy: *Hey TeeTee! How you been? I haven't heard from you in awhile. I'm just now seeing your message. I was in the shower. Long day at the office. Call me now. I'm available.*

No time was wasted by Tamron to make the call.

"Hello!" Landy answered.

"Hey, cuz. It's a pleasure to hear your voice again."

"It's a pleasure to hear yours as well. What took you so long to contact me?"

"I've been super busy, cuz. I really have. But nonetheless, we're here now."

"Indeed, we are. So, what's this you really need to speak with me about?"

Tamron exhaled heavily. This signaled to Landy that she probably needed to brace herself for something of serious nature to come her way. Tamron proceeded with what she wanted to say to her cousin.

"Look, cuz. You remember my boyfriend Montell, don't you?"

"Of course. How could I forget him and all those stories you related to me about the both of you? It's been a while since I last had a chance to see him or heard you speak about him. But yeah... I remember Montell. And is he still locked up?"

"No. He's not. Well... actually... he got out about a year ago from the time you talking about. But recently, he got arrested again. That's why I'm calling you now, cuz. It's about him."

"Well damn! Who has this nucca scammed now? He is a real con artist, I know. But what's going on with dude?"

Tamron exhaled once more. "It's serious this time, cuz. So serious that I really don't wanna say. But I have to. Because I'm now looking to hire you to be his lawyer."

"Tamron! Are you serious?! You mean to tell me, Montell went away to prison and did all that damn time, he finally gets out, ain't even home a good year yet, and he's back in trouble already? Ain't no way! Did the two of you even have the chance to fuck good while he was out? Because I'm busy trying to understand what the hell is it he's got on you, to have you all caught up with him and entangled in his shit?"

"I'mma say it like this for you, cuz. And I really hope you can relate. When you love somebody, you love somebody. That's the best answer I can give you on that. But to be honest, I don't believe that Montell did any of the things that they saying he has done."

"And exactly, what's that, might I ask?"

"Huh," she released. "They tryna say he raped and killed somebody. But I—"

"Wait a damn minute... What?!" Landy retorted, cutting Tamron's words off in doing so.

"The police is saying that he raped and then murdered some white chick. She was somebody he was once involved with," Tamron came back with.

"I know muthafucking well it better not be that same white girl he was cheating on you with?! Not the one you forgave him over when he came running back to you with all those weak ass apologies, is it?"

"Yes, Landy. Her. The same white girl, Mandy Barfield. But that's not the point. What *is* the point, is that... Montell ain't did no shit like that! He ain't no fuckin' rapist! And ain't never had to take no pussy! And besides, the girl was pregnant too. So more than likely, the baby was Montell's seed."

"Okay. So, my question to you now is... If this really be so... Why you so intent on having his problems yours to deal with too? That's what I wanna know? Why not just leave him be, to deal with his own problems? Why not stay away like you are now and not involve yourself?" Landy asked in her four-fold thread of questions to her cousin.

"It's because Landy... I really don't believe that Montell did it. And I can't abandon him like that. I can't just up and haul ass on him without so much as offering some type of help. And besides, Montell took really good care of me, before he first went to prison, and once he got out. Also, I wouldn't be the boss-bitch I proclaim myself to be these days, and I wouldn't have the type of money I now got, had it not been for Montell. So, the least a bitch could do is, get the man a fuckin' lawyer. But look," Tamron's patience begun to run thin behind the questioning Landy had and her display of dislike she verbally expressed towards Montell, "you want the job... Or you don't? You willing to represent my man in this situation. Or do I need to get busy tryna find another lawyer who will?" Tamron was emphatic with what she had to say.

In the background, Landy could be heard pecking away in a professional manner at the keys on her laptop. She was apparently researching the case that Montell was a wanted man on, but now in custody. "What's his whole name again, now?" she asked of Tamron.

"His full name on record is Montell-Jermaine-McNeal. And I assume you looking up every, right?"

"Mm-hmm, I am," responded Landy.

"The case originated in Hall County Georgia. But he recently was arrested in—"

"Philadelphia. I see it now," Landy cut in to say.

"Right."

"And I also see he got shot, or something like that."

"I can't even begin to tell you what that was all about. But I'll know more once me and him finally do talk," Tamron let out. "How long you think it'll be before they get him back down here?"

"Two weeks maybe... Three weeks... Possibly a month. Depending. But if he was to just simply go ahead with it and waive extradition, he'll save himself the hassle of the process. It's nothing but identification determination anyways. And according to what I'm now reading, that's not an issue to be debated."

"Right... Right. That's understandable."

"But look, Tamron. These some *'serious'* fucking charges this *ninja* of yours got to go up against the state with."

"I'm aware of that. But what's the ticket, Landy? Just tell me that, is all I now need to know right now?"

"Honestly, this gonna run y'all two anywhere between a hundred and fifty to two hundred thousand dollars as a retainer fee to represent your dude on this case. Maybe more, once I consult about it," Landy stated. She attempted to make it sound grim in a way, hoping that Tamron would back out and try to go get a cheaper lawyer. "Y'all got that kinda money available?"

"Bitch, please! That and more! And how you wanna be paid? I can take care of it however you like! I got it!"

Chapter 29

Back In Philly...

The family of Roderick couldn't seem to catch a break from having their loved ones continue to fall as victims to violent clashes they found themselves caught up in. With Roderick himself being the latest casualty, he felt privileged to simply still be alive. Especially so, after the way that the two—he and Montell—were ambushed by those hitters. Roderick will have to go through tremendous series of physical therapy sessions just to gain a minute level of semblance in mobility he once enjoyed before being shot. He was still mean as a rattlesnake though, a side of him no one never knew existed, not even him, until it was time to become this way. His mind was set on having his people gain some form of get-back at the first available opportunity that they have. Somebody got to get it, he reasoned.

Now home and healing from the wounds he suffered, Roderick had Big Xav there with him, two of his brothers on his dad's side, (Harvey and Jarvis) Yammy the soldier of Big Xav, Jamie had flown in to check on him, and Lea was there too. They were all inside the master bedroom of one of the homes that A-One left to Roderick. A discussion was being held over the incident and who the perpetrators were.

In a low voice, Roderick spoke out to them. To Big Xav first. "Them niggaz got me, Big Homie. They caught me down bad, Xav. But I respect it though. This how the game goes, ain't it?"

"Damn, Rod," Xav let out. It's fucked up to see you in this predicament, lil homie. But I promise you, we gonna hit back, and hit back hard when we do. And we managed to get all the information we needed to know who got you and your homie. It was that slime-ass nigga, Khalib and his people. They so-called themselves striking back behind the uncle of theirs being hit."

"So Khalib... he the same cat who was on the phone that day poppin' all that smack, huh?" asked Roderick.

"Exactly! He's the one. And I ain't gonna stop 'til I personally eat this nigga! Even if that mean by myself!"

"Aye... Just do what you gotta do. But whatever it is y'all do, just don't let that bitch-nigga get away, or the two niggaz who actually pulled the trigger on me and my homie, Montell!"

"We gonna all be sure we handle this, bro," said Roderick's sibling Harvey, as he Chime in to speak on the subject.

"That's word on that bro," uttered Jarvis, the other male sibling present.

Lea was reduced to tears at the sight of her crippled baby brother. "I'm sorry that this happened to you, bro. I really am. We gonna make it right for you, though. For everybody else too," she said.

"Shit, y'all better! And not a day should pass where y'all not looking to track them niggaz down. Because A-One and Boo-Man need payback too. Bro's bodyguard-homie need us to stand up for him too," Roderick let out.

Jamie finally spoke up. "Rod... What the fuck, bro! Man, I really hate to see you like this, homie. We still got a lot of business to be handled in the world bro, and we need you present to turn up with us. Shit, Seduction City, ain't gonna be the same without you there, nigga. On everything, it ain't."

Roderick smiled. A thought passed through his mind. "I can see that nigga Geno now, Jamie. He hatin' like a muthafucka,' ain't he? Because one less of us mean one-up for him, don't it?"

"You shouldn't even be thinking that way, Rod. Because no matter what, I'mma continue to stand on business for you, me, and Mo. I definitely got us when it comes to what we own in Seduction City," Jamie adamantly stated.

Everyone rotated their head from each person talking to the person being spoken to between exchanges. Roderick spoke up once more.

"Speakin' of Mo... What's up with him?"

Jamie said, "From what I know, they booked him here in Philly, once he was let go from the hospital. He's gonna be extradited back down south soon, if he haven't already by now."

"What's your homie's name, bro?" asked Lea. "I can call over to the county jail and check on the website to see what's his status."

"Jamie, give my sister Mo's credentials, if you don't mind," Roderick asked of the friend.

Lea was provided everything necessary to perform a check on Montell. "The website says he's still here in Philly, bro. They got him at **CFCF.** I'mma call now to be sure. Sometimes the website don't be updated," she let out.

Roderick talked more. "But on the business side of things, Xav, how's everything looking? And of course, I ain't able to lead no more, so y'all gonna have to continue and move on with both my brothers there," he pointed by rotating his eyes from Harvey to Jarvis

The two siblings equally looked on at Big Xav and awaited his response.

Big Xav said, "A'ight, so, all the houses, cars, and businesses A-One left behind, I don't know nothing too much about, other than y'all Pop and you Rod, got control over. But as far as the street business is concerned... the plug was ready to move out with you on everything, and then, this shit happened to you, right at the point of everything beginning to settle in the aftermath of the situation that took A-One away from us. It's like, these two incidents, took place too close together. I had the meeting and all set up for you with the plug. But now... we gotta hit the reset button and start all over again. And at the same time, I don't even know how y'all feel or thinking." He waved a pointed finger at everybody present. "But with me... this will be a never-ending beef between that family and the one I'm a part of. I ain't gonna ever let this go! Every chance I get, I'mma see to it that a body drop of a family member of this nigga who's marked for death. This nigga Khalib. That's on what *God* loves, homie!" Big Xav vehemently spat. He now had tears in his eyes and boiling blood racing through his veins. The emotions ran down the left cheek of his. The memory of A-One was in full effect. Big Xav's adrenaline rush. He was eager to execute a solid measure of vengeance.

Silence surrounded the room. No one uttered a word for maybe a good sixty seconds. The words of Big Xav resonate deeply. His voice held weight.

Finally, the elder of the siblings there, Harvey, spoke up once more. "Ain't no need to worry, Rod. Me, Jarvis, Lea, Big Xav, and the rest of the family who's in the streets with it, we're very well capable of re-establishing our camp and get back to having motion again. We all just gotta come to the table and make a decision on who the head of the group should be. And this shouldn't be a hard thing to do. But in the meantime, all we need you to do is rest up, bro." Harvey laid a hand on Roderick's head and stroked his hair forward, going with the grain. "And don't trouble yourself or concern yourself with none of the street shit no more. And get well soon. We here with you. That's it."

Everyone else nodded in agreement to all that Harvey had said.

The talk between them all continued on a little longer before everybody but Lea, went about their separate ways.

Big Xav made a solid point in the long drawn out statement he'd made "... *this will be a never ending beef....*" He couldn't have been more honest or more correct than that. Under no other circumstances could he have. The street war would continue.

Chapter 30

In The Meantime...

Over in Princeton, New Jersey, Tiffany was staying at Verena's house with Verena's mother Mrs. Deanne, and looking after the twins, until Verena was mentally well enough to have a judge sign off to an order granting her release from the Trenton Psychiatrist Hospital in Trenton, New Jersey, the place she's was being held. Her suicide attempt turned out to be a far more troubling cry for help than she originally thought it to be. And if her intentions was to not actually kill herself but was rather to get attention, she did a very good job at this. She'd gotten *all* the attention she wanted, but the kind that she hadn't thought possible when she pulled her little *"I'm gonna kill myself"* stunt.

Verena's stay was now at the three-week mark and counting. It was an ongoing psychological adventure of some sort. Her body was being pumped daily with anti-depressants and other tranquilizing type sedatives. To make matters worse for the once highly intelligent high-ranking state of Georgia official, everything prescribed to her by the asylum doctor charged with overseeing her, was on an involuntary basis. She had no choice in the matter. And if she refused, she'd be restrained by the facility's handlers and injected by force. Her refusal would also compel the judge assigned over her case, to push back on an order to release her. So, for everything that was not in Verena's control (a position she hated with a passion to be in) she was forced to endure. There were no other options.

Verena was allowed a non-contact visit from family by the facility. Her Mother and Tiffany paid her a visit. Yes, the twins were brought along as well. Erica and Eric, Jr) They resembled their daddy so much that the very thought of how her resentfulness and how much she despised Eric did actually pass through the mind of Tiffany.

She silently questioned within, *I wonder will 'Rena's hatred and bitterness towards Eric have any effect on how she'll treat the kids, once she's finally let out of here? Because she does have an ax to grind. And for all those who's on the wrong side of that ax, surely will have hell to pay.*

These and other random thoughts happen to pass through Tiffany's mind as they awaited Verena to be brought into the phone booth style visitation cubicle.

Shortly thereafter, in walked Verena, flanked on both sides by two male handlers and handcuffed at the front. She was let inside the thick glass encased booth and locked there to have her visit. With her left hand Verena grabbed the phone from the hook it was stationed, and with her right hand spread wide, she pressed the palm flat against the glass, as if she was palming the hand of her daughter and her son, one after another. The smile disappeared, then came the emotion. Verena begun to cry like she never had before.

The Mother, Mrs. Deanne was the first to left the receiver from the hook on their side of the glass and metal box. "'Rena... how you holding up, baby? Everything been going good with you?" she asked, gazing heavily at Verena's appearance to make a determination of her own as to her daughter's mental, physical, and spiritual well-being.

Still experiencing an emotional release, Verena eventually responded," Momma I'm ready to leave this place and go home," she let out. Thick strings of cobwebs stretch from her top lip and the roof of her mouth to the bottom portion. "Why they still holding me here? I made one bad decision... one that I was eventually able to bounce back from. But they keep treating me like I'm some type of serial killer of some sort. They keep giving me all this medication every day and a shot at least once a week. For what?! I'm okay now, Momma. This has to end."

"And it will. Soon. Me and Tiffany got you a lawyer. She's the same one who represented Tiffany in family court to help her be granted temporary custody of your babies here," Mrs. Deanne said, gesturing to the toddlers with a nod of the head and a point of the finger. "The lawyer said that the police and others made her aware that because of what you've done, it was only procedure, and that you shouldn't be here for no more than thirty days at best. But she told me to tell you that you gotta stop fighting with the staff here, and that she'll be here to see you this week coming up, and she's gonna do all necessary in seeing to it that you're out of here soon."

"Soon like, once these damn thirty days come to an end, right?"

"Right. It's been eighteen days already, so you just hang in there, okay. And stop fighting with these people too. That's not gonna help you get home any faster. And I still don't know the whole story behind what happened with you and Eric. That bastard hasn't so much as showed up to the house not once to check on his own kids or to check with me to know how you was doing. But that's another story all by itself. I don't even wanna get you all worked up again about it either."

"I'm moving on from Eric, Momma. Life is gonna go on without him. It's gonna have to. And once I turn over all of the information I have on him from the private investigator I hired, he's gonna really be sorry he ever abandoned me and my babies. I'm taking his ass to child support court and all! Watch! And the federal government and the Atlanta Police, gonna wanna have a talk with that negro too. I did give him a fair warning, Momma. Lord knows, I did. I even went so far as to give him an ultimatum... to either be back with me, our babies, and inside our household... or... to go on and be with that little *'Mexican peasant'* he's been cheating with. But he chose her and walked away on me with her. So now, his ass has hell to pay. Simple and plain!"

" 'Rena, don't get yourself stressed out all over again with that on your mind, baby. Please. Don't. Just get him away from your thoughts and be ready to come home soon. That's all Momma needs you to do. Now here... talk to your sister for a moment before we have to go. We don't get but thirty minutes to visit you, so."

Mrs. Deanne passed Tiffany the phone at that point. Tiffany was holding Eric Jr and Mrs. Deanne held Erica. Both of Verena's babies recognized her. They made faint attempts to reach out to her, eager to be held by her, as she always would do. Even with Verena draped in a facility all white jumpsuit and her hair frayed and uncared for, the twins still knew that indeed, it was their Mommy present who they looked on at beyond the glass.

Tiffany put the phone up to her ear. "Hey, 'Rena."

"Hey, sis. And before we say anything else, please let me say this much. I thank you and I love you, for stepping in and helping out Momma with the kids and all, okay. You're a Godsend, sis."

"You're welcome, and I appreciate your words. But how you holding up?"

"I'm doing much better now, since I was allowed this visit from y'all, and I have the chance to see my babies. But... this too shall pass. And I'll be back home soon."

"You're so right about that sis... *'this too shall pass'*... and you'll be home soon."

"Thank you for responding in time and saving my life, Tiffany. I don't know what had gotten into me, sis. I really don't.

The damn devil! Tiffany thought on, but didn't feel the need to verbalize this. She was more in line with the Christian notion that *if anyone ever develops the ill-notion in mind that they should kill themselves, that it's demonic in totality, and nothing but the work of Satan.*

"I don't blame you for none of this, 'Rena. It's all Eric's fault. He pushed you to this, and the same type of energy that he's put out there, shall be the same to come back to him. Karma... as they say... *always* hit back. She never misses," Tiffany expressed.

"That's so true... that's so true. But on another note... my babies... they not too much to deal with, are they?" Verena asked, making a light sense of humor to take over a sensitive subject dealing with Eric.

"Oh, noooo. These two here are angels, girl. And I love 'em!" Tiffany then planted a kiss on the cheeks of the twins, Erica first.

"They sho' can eat, can't they?" More humor laced between the lines of reality from Verena. "And when they want what they want, they cut-up about it, won't they?" she let out with a slight laugh at the end of her words.

"Girl... what you talking about. Especially this one right here," meaning Erica. "But I understand though. She gets it from her Momma, huh." The humor proceeded.

Verena smiled brightly at Tiffany's accurate remark of her daughter. "I know that's right. And baby girl definitely ain't afraid to let you know either."

They continued on in making small, pleasant conversation throughout the remainder of the visit. Tiffany and Mrs. Deanne passed the phone back and forth to one another. They both knew that so long as Verena was laughing, smiling, being cheerful, and expressing an uplifted spirit, that God knows, she was okay. She definitely showed all the signs of having some semblance of recovery in the aftermath of her psychological unhinging.

The thirty minutes were nearly up. Verena mentioned something to Tiffany about her needing to get in contact with a private detective female for her. Someone she'd long hired. The detective's name was Montania, but Monti for short.

Verena told Tiffany to relate the facts to Monti about her ongoing situation and her current whereabouts. From there, Monti is to provide Tiffany with everything that she's gathered on Eric thus far. The work would continue. In addition, Tiffany is to get $15,000 out of the safe Verena has located in her home bedroom and hand it over to Monti as payment to proceed with the type of work Verena hired her to do.

Monti was one of three detectives who owned and operated the firm, *Beyond the Surface Private Investigative Services, Inc,* and the only African-American along side a white female and a White male colleague.

The firm charged $800 per week. And more than likely, Verena, would be released from the asylum long before the seven weeks of work prepaid for would come to an end. From there, Verena and Monti would contact the appropriate authorities, so to hand Eric whatever measure of justice and karma that he'd already had coming, according to Verena.

Verena said, "You're gonna have to get Monti's phone number outta the contacts in my phone, okay," she stated, providing Tiffany the seven digit passcode to unlock the Apple iPhone Pro. It was actually the digits to the birthday of the twins.

"Gotcha, 'Rena. I'll be sure to take care of this for you, sis. And one more thing from me before we go," Tiffany mumbled into the receiver.

"What's that?"

"It's about something and someone totally different than what we've talked about already."

Verena jarred her head then furrowed her eyebrows. She kinda sorta, sorta kinda had a hunch as to what it possibly was and of who it possibly was, that Tiffany wanted to mention to her. She'd uttered something of similar importance before. And judging by Verena's body language and expression, she felt that what it was about then, it's about now.

"I'm listening," Verena let out.

Tiffany proceeded, "I don't know what this information is worth to you these days, but for *whatever* it's worth... your old boyfriend—Montell—was injured really bad in a shooting incident. And to add further insult to injury, how about, the very moment the man is released from the hospital, he gets arrested and was taken to the county jail."

Mrs. Deanne had no knowledge on who they were talking about. She never heard the name *Montell* mentioned before as being a boyfriend of Verena's. So, she simply sat and allowed the two girls to talk more on the private matter.

"Oh, yeah! Damn! As much as he hates being incarcerated... I feel sorry for him. I really do.

Yeah right, bitch! I bet you do! And you're only saying this and trying to sound all nice about it now because you know that you made a bad choice in picking Eric over Montell. So now, you're regretting it. But as the old saying goes, you reap what you sow, thought Tiffany.

"Me, too," Tiffany remarked behind Verena.

Verena actually had the audacity to think that the snitching she'd done out of spite against Eric, Montell, Jamie, and Roderick, about the income tax scams and the other white collar crimes that she had knowledge of that they'd committed, to include her also into the mix, had finally been executed by the IRS, with Montell being the first of the four to fall. She sat and awaited confirmation on all she'd speculated. However, the same way that she's never the one to rush to judge someone, Tiffany didn't rush to blurt out what for, Montell gotten arrested on. After all, only days before Montell and Roderick were ambushed and nearly killed, in a serious beef that Montell had absolutely nothing to do with, he and Tiffany had been intimate and fucked like newlyweds in a hotel suite downtown Center City Philly.

Verena then asked," if anything, what for? What was Montell arrested for?" She was attempting to sound all poetic and polite, so to get Tiffany to give up the tea

However, with Tiffany, already in the know on how phony Verena was and could make herself not appear with certain dramas, but actually was, didn't give her the satisfaction in knowing that Montell was booked on the type serious violent felonies he now faced. Therefore, Tiffany lied.

"You know what... I have no idea myself on what for. I just heard his name mentioned through the grapevine, is all," responded Tiffany.

"Oh. You don't say. How interesting that is."

The visit was concluded on this note.

Chapter 31

Months Earlier...

Beyond the Surface Private Investigative Services was contacted by a Verena Evette Gordon, in the early morning hours on this particular day. It was a Tuesday, 8:00 a.m. The office had just opened. Montania Elaine Owens, as always, was the first to arrive, and more than likely, would be the last to leave. She absolutely loved the work that she did, and often though of herself as a real life *Holly Gibney,* the fascinating and recluse-like private detective created by famous author Stephen King.

Monti had read and seriously studied any and all books of the fiction author that featured Holly in them, especially the *Bill Hodges Trilogy—Mr. Mercedes... Finders Keepers...* and *End of Watch.* Monti was obsessed with Holly and sought to model herself after the character and live similar to how Holly did in her fictional world. But the breadth and depth of which Mr. King has written his Holly featured stories, was made more realistic than Monti could imagine. No one could tell her that Holly wasn't an actual *person.* They'd probably have a fight on their hands had they done so.

But Monti, was slim, with a wasp-like waistline, slightly tall for a female at five foot nine, was always casually dressed like today in *Lululemon* attire—hat, tee shirt, multi-pocket cargo pants, and a matching pair of Vans sneakers on her feet. She wore a natural low cut kinky hairstyle that had a razor-sharp all-around lineup about it, two three-inch parts at both the right and left temples and was an all-natural female of 27 years of age. No lipstick, no makeup, no fake hair ... absolutely nothing was artificially assimilated about her.

Monti picked up the landline phone on the second ring. Verena was encouraged to contact Monti by a sorority sister of hers. They were members of the Order of The Eastern Star. An aunt of Monti's actually. She'd recommended Verena hit up her niece about the troubles with her significant other she was experiencing.

"Beyond The Surface Private Investigative Services! This is Montania. How may I help you?"

"Yes, hello! I'm Verena."

"Thanks for your call, Verena," Monti responded.

"My pleasure. And I was actually given the contact information to this service by a dear friend of mine. Her name is Shurvon Clarkston. She specifically told me to ask for you, Montania," Verena said.

"Yes, Aunt Shurvon. She's the best. And please, just call me Monti. It's easier on the tongue." A sense of humor was expressed to make Verena feel comfortable.

They shared a light laugh at the witty remark.

"I'm glad you called, Verena. How may I be of service to you?"

Verena let out a hard sigh. It sounded almost as if she was present on her first day of psycho-therapy with a psychiatrist of her liking and she was the eager to vent to. She said," I have a very stressful and complicated situation on my hands I'm dealing with, Monti. And I'm so ready to find out everything I can and on what I need to know, so I can eventually be done with it."

"Well ... whatever the situation may be, Verena, I'm more than sure that we can help. And since you were referred to us by my aunt, this has to be a personal and touchy situation you're having to endure?"

"It is. Because it can't be cured. And the only other options is to just endure it. But not any longer."

"Relate the basis of the issues for me please?" Monti encouraged Verena.

She exhaled hard again. "Where do I start? I simply don't know." Verena choke up front emotions in this instance. "But ... the ... *'boyfriend'* of mine ... I feel so ashamed to refer to him as this, being the type of woman I am and the stature of a lady I worked so hard to become, he hasn't been a faithful participant in the relationship that we have. And again, Monti, I feel *so* ashamed to speak like this about a man who I have carried on a relationship with for more than a year now, and we're nice even married yet."

"I'm not in the business of being judgmental, Verena, nor am I in the business of forming any opinion on a matter. I'm here to be of help to you. And at all cost, I'm gonna do nothing but the best of work that I could, in seeing to it that you receive a sufficient outcome, the kind that you came to us with the expectations of having," Monti made clear to Verena.

"And I thank you for this, Monti. Because trust and reliance, is the two things a woman like me need most right about now."

"Now ... this significant other that you speak of ... do you two have any kids together?"

Verena didn't want to say, so Monti said it for her.

With a bit more of shame spread across her face, Verena reluctantly answered," yeah, we do. Twins actually."

"And what is it you would like to employ our services on in this regard? How is the father of your kids causing you trouble?" *No matter what the situation is with the client, be professional at all times.* The words of Monti's criminal defense lawyer Aunt Sylvia—the sister of Monti's mother and her aunt Shurvon— came to mind.

"For starters, I have strong reasons to believe that he's seeing someone else. I've taken notice of all the signs and red flags that I needed to see to know this much. I just haven't had the chance to catch it yet." This was before the incident Eric had with Roderick Atlantic City and the court appearance where Eric was accomplished by Joleena and Verena eventually caught him red-handed cheating.

"So basically, you need for us to do as our namesake and dig *beyond the surface,* so to ascertain the facts about this affair that your spouse is having? Is this what you need us to do, Verena?"

"Yes! Absolutely!" she stated emphatically. "Ascertain the facts for me. That's a very good word choice of yours there. I like that. And I need less people as possible in my business, please. Is this possible?"

"Yes, Verena. Yes, it is."

"Thank you! When can we meet?"

"We could meet today if you like. And I'm sure you know where our office is located, correct?"

"I do. It's in Trenton, right?"

"Right," Monti let out in reply. She then went on to provide Verena with the address of the office for purpose of GPS.

"Joe soon are you available?"

"As soon as you need me to be, Verena. I'm on your side. And together, we shall get the results that you're look for throughout this trying time you're going through." *Make the client feel comfortable. Tell them all the things you know that they want to hear, but without raising the level of expectations between you and the client.* More of the gospel of Aunt Sylvia passed through Monti's mind, following another maxim of hers quoted in Monti's head.

"That's perfect. And if anything, what personal effects of the significant others do you have?" asked Monti.

How come I couldn't think to call Eric's ass my significant other at first when we began this call, as opposed to referring to this nucca as my goddamn 'boyfriend? thought Verena.

"I have everything, Monti. Everything that you may need," related Verena. She continued, "Me and this man were *supposed* to have gotten married, Monti. But obviously, this wasn't longer any part of his outlook on life."

"If you will, Verena, just hold on to all you have to say to me about this man until we meet later today. Okay."

"Yes, Monti. This I'll do. But I'll be there in the next hour."

"Sounds perfect. See you then."

"Uh-huh. You, too."

The call between the two came to an end.

***

One Hour Later...

Ever eager to get straight to business, Verena didn't waste a minute of time getting to Trenton to meet Monti, upon dropping off the twins at the daycare. Mrs. Deanne was taken to the flower shop to open for the day.

Upon entering the office of the firm, Verena was greeted by the two esteemed colleague co-owners of Monti. It was Watley Coggins and Amanda Vickers.

With a smiling face, Amanda states," Hello, ma'am! Welcome to Beyond the Surface."

"It's a pleasure to be here. I'm to meet with Monti, please," responded Verena.

"Sure. I'll let her know right away that she has a client here to see her."

"Let her know it's *Verena,* please."

"I sure will," Amanda came back with, then picked up the phone to notify Monti.

The office of the firm resembled one that lawyers would have, but a tad smaller. Verena took a seat in one of the plush leather chairs in the lobby. She had a second look inside her tote bag she carries at the personal effects of Eric's that Monti encouraged her to bring. There was a copy of both, Georgia and New Jersey, driver's licenses; a copy of his Social Security card; a copy of his Birth Certificate, and a print-out of his criminal record from the Bureau of Prisons, amongst other things.

"I believe this should be enough for now, to at least get things started," she murmured to herself.

The bag was closed once more, leaving her to have a look at her phone. Nothing from Eric. He'd been out all night had become a norm for him now. Another outing with the young Hispanic sensation, Joleena. This was weeks after the trip to the Big Apple that the two had enjoyed. Things begun to heat up, in the fire and fury of lust between them, and in the level of scorn and hurt that Verena began to experience.

The conference call that Monti was on finally ended. She appeared from her office to physically meet and greet Verena. For a moment, Verena was stunned to know that Monti was a full fledged African American female, one that was almost as black as the ink in a *Pental* RSVP BK91 pen. This brought about a level of comfort for Verena.

She's a sista, Verena thought, as she looked at the ebony complexion of skin the private eye had. *She's dark and naturally like me.*

Judging by Monti's voice over the phone call, and by the way she so eloquently pronounced and enunciated her words, Verena could have sworn to God that the young lady was of one of two distinctions: either she was a mixed female, in this scenario, having a black mother and a white father who was of high intelligence and thoroughly educated, growing up amongst privileged and entitled white kids; or, was a really light-skinned African American, who wanted nothing to do with her black race, and especially, nothing to do with her ethnicity, being also from a privileged and entitled background herself. Monti was nothing of the two. And in due time, Verena would eventually know all of this of what she needed to know about her.

The eyes of the two met. Verena stood to her feet. She knew this was the investigator that she'd come to relate her *"boyfriend"* issues to. Besides, the name tag on the wall next to the office door of Monti's read: **MONTANIA** *"Meow"* **OWENS**, a play on her actual government name, Montania Elaine Owens.

"Verena?" spoke Monti.

"I am," she replied, then politely approached to shake the hand of the potential newfound friend.

"Right this way, please," Monti encouraged with the extension of her left hand for Verena to be welcomed into her office. She smiled as well.

Verena reciprocated with both the smile and the energy.

Inside the office there was only one chair for guests. It was situated opposite Monti's. "Pleas, have a seat, and let's dig into the issues that seem to be plaguing you emotionally."

"Let's do this, shall we. Because for far too long now, this one main issue has grown more ill and caused more issues. They're all connected."

"I see. So, for starters, your significant other ... what's his name?" asked Monti.

"It's Eric. His name is Eric."

"Okay. Now, give me two main errors in your eyes, that Eric has done, to give you reason to believe that he's been of bad behavior in regard to the relationship you two share?"

"—*Supposed* to be sharing. There's a big difference. But the only thing that he seems to be sharing these days is himself. To answer your question though, what has he done to give me reason to believe that he's no good?"

"I need two reasons, if you will."

"Okay, for one, when we first moved here to New Jersey from Georgia, I was six months pregnant with our babies, and he was there with me daily, making doctor's appointments alongside me, and being the ideal expectant of a father that I needed him to be. And then, everything changed a few weeks before I hosted my baby shower. He begun talking to me in a very disrespectful manner; he started staying out later and later into the night until he eventually wouldn't come home at all most nights now from that point. Not until the next morning after when the sun was up and he'd go to his man space of the house to sleep and repeat the process the next night. That's one major issue he's brought to our relationship."

Monti speed wrote down notes on a writing pad. She paused to ask a question. "Verena, in order for me to better help you moving forward, I need to record this meeting. Are you okay with this?"

"That's fine by me. Do all you need to do so that we can know all that there's to know."

Monti tapped the icon on her phone to audio record. She verbalized all that she'd previously wrote out. Attention was put back on Verena at this point.

"Okay. What was the other issue you wanted to make me aware of?"

Verena answered," His neglect of the kids. That's not how a father is to treat his toddlers. We have a son and a daughter together."

Monti continued to let her ink pen dance atop the yellow-colored notebook. Everything was written in blue. "Okay. I got all that. And I know exactly what I need to do to uncover what it is you're desiring to know."

"—What does he have going behind the scenes... With whom... For how long have this been going on... And exactly where does the two stay when they get together? These are the things that I want to know. What's the retainer fee to hire you?" Verena asked, now eager to get the process officially moving.

"For this line of Investigative work, it'll be $800 weekly."

Verena brought out her checkbook and wrote for a payment of $5,000 to the firm. She asked a question before handing over the check. "So, for clarity, it'll be you and only you doing the work for me, right? No one else?"

"It‹ll be me and only me. But say for instance, if I were to need any assistance from my two colleagues in there," she pointed in the direction of the lobby, "then I will notice you beforehand to make you aware of this, the importance of why they would be needed, and get your permission to have them assist."

Verena looked sternly into the eyes of Monti. "I can agree to these terms. But if you will, Monti, please, I'm a very private person, because I'm a very private person, and wish to keep my business out of the know of as many people as I possibly could."

"That's understandable, Verena. And this, will do," Monti assured her, now extending her hand to receive the check at this point and maintaining her signature detective demeanor the whole time.

Chapter 32

One week after the initial meeting between Verena and Monti, and the payment for the services neighbor made, Monti was already making serious progress in keeping track of Eric and his movement and said activities. Verena consented to allow Monti have someone place a tracker underneath the body of Eric's Durango SUV. Monti was now able to keep tabs on him by GPS. Shocking revelations begun to come to the light little-by-little.

Being that the work Monti's firm conducted was a quasi version of detective work that true law enforcement officials themselves performed, by law and by penalty of imprisonment, if the agency were to discover any crimes that is being committed or have been committed while investigating a matter for any of their clients, or, that the commission of any crimes currently taking place, everything has to be reported to the appropriate way. Without fail.

Therefore, when the fact was revealed that Monti that Eric was heavily into narcotics trafficking, were being supplied by the Diaz family (a notorious distribution carrier for the violent and often murderous Sinaloa Cartel of Mexico and had developed and affair with the daughter of the infamous Oscar Diaz) Monti knew without doubt that she couldn't take the criminal aspects of Eric's philandering to Verena at no point, but instead, had to report this to high law enforcement, because local authorities wasn't sufficient enough to deal with this particular criminal cell. The Diaz clan, proved to be a different kinda animal altogether. The feds needed to be notified.

This wasn't the first time that Monti had came across criminal endeavors being carried out by the subject(s) of her minute private investigations. However, this may prove to be the most significant of them all, prompting her to contact a male acquaintance of hers who was a member of the DEA. This was a guy she'd dated in the past. They'd met on a chance happen occasion. On a case she'd been working, coincidentally, regarding a beloved dog that was presumed missing, but had actually gotten kidnapped for ransom by a rival drug dealer.

Quentin Lovett still had strong feelings for Monti, and seemed to be forever in the habit of wanting to continue and show her exactly how he felt about her. The two still talked on the phone from time-to-time, and Monti would even consent to date him more on certain occasions. But a committed relationship was the thing that Quentin wanted, and Monti, wasn't quite ready for this just yet, because she was still grieving the passing of her mother four years after the fact, and keeping busy with her line of work, was the only thing that kept away the stress and the depression.

Also, in Monti's own words, she said that *"her duty to work and her clients, needed and deserved her time more than a man did."* Nonetheless, Quentin was still optimistic about the future and them eventually being a couple.

Monti contacted Quentin to provide him the details of a potential case that could aid him with a promotion within the Bureau. The tall stylish Morris Chestnut looking, goatee wearing, immaculate bald-head, well-groomed and physically fit brother took the call. The day was an off-day of his; a Saturday. Monti knew his schedule fairly well. He was off every other weekend and she also knew he wouldn't mind hearing from her. It had been a couple of weeks since the last he had.

He answered," Well, my-my, ain't I glad to hear from you. How nice it is."

"*Aren't* you glad to hear from me. And yes, how nice it must be for you," Monti responded. "And I see I'm still a contact in your phone."

"You are. For all the right reasons too. And yes, I stand corrected. You know my Southern grammar takes over my mode of speech every now and then. I'm from Yamesee, South Carolina, and I have to let this show at times," he said and continued to smile into the camera lens of the phone.

Monti reciprocated with a warm smile of her own and showing teeth with it. "You're good, country boy. Actually, I like it when your Gullah-Geechee side comes out. It reminds me of how much in-tune with that side of yourself that you are."

"Thank you. But what's up? You hit me up at ten in the A.M. And whatever it is, I'm sure that it has to have a level of importance to it."

"It does. And in fact, this could potentially be some information you could use to build a case and advance you in rank, once you see it through the proper channels."

"Is that right? Who are the subjects that one of your investigations have stumbled upon?"

"Does the Diaz family name ring a bell for you?"

"It sure does. They're an extension of the Sinaloa Cartel based here in the Northeast portion of the country. We've been slowly gathering information for the longest on them and the criminal enterprise that they operate. But everything seems to always turn out to be a dead end, or either, the informants who we rely on to give us information on them so to paint a better picture of what their world looks like on the inside, always turns up dead or missing, never to be found and presumed dead anyway."

"That was until now."

"Oh really! And what is it you got that will help put me and my colleagues one step closer to taking down the Diaz family?"

Monti then went on to relate her business that she has with Verena and the particular tricks of the trade that she'd put to use to keep track of Eric for her.

"So, not only is this *Eric* guy having an affair with the princess of the Diaz clan, he's being supplied narcotics by them; he's in bed with them on other businesses as well; and he frequents the home of the ringleader often... Oscar Diaz? Is this what you're telling me?" asked Quentin, in total astonishment at how easy the information came to him without so much work having to be done to obtain it.

"This is exactly what I'm saying to you, Quentin. Because by me being bound by the law, I have no choice but to report any and all crimes that's brought to my attention through the investigations of each and every case that I take on."

"Look, Monti, are you free to meet today?"

"I *might* be. So long as you're willing to treat me to something nice, I am. It's *'Quid Pro Quo'* Quentin. Something for something."

"I like the sound of that. So, it's a date for us, huh?"

"If that's what you wanna call it." She smiled into the lens of the camera exuberantly. "I simply call it, a *'friend meeting with a friend to have a conversation'* about the line of work we do. But over a cocktail or two," she let out with a smile.

"That's what's up. So, I'll see you at say, six- *ish*... Seven-*ish?"*

"You can pick me up at seven, Quentin. And it's only a casual outing for us, okay. No need to dress to the *nines* like you're prone to do."

Monti maintained a bright smile, while at the same time advising Quentin, that what they would be doing later in the evening, wouldn't require him to appear so formal in clothing. Having been in the Bureau for the years he had, taught Quentin the value and necessity to stay presentable at all times relevant. And the notion, he took it seriously.

"I'll be there at six-fifty," he responded with a smile of his own and causing the same reaction from her at his remark.

The call ended, and the two continued with what they were doing prior to, with the eagerness and desire now in play, at seeing each other in the next few hours to come.

Chapter 33

Presently...

Montell was still being held in the county jail in Philly now, two weeks after being released from the hospital. He was scheduled to appear before a judge on the issue of extradition in the next week to come. But for the time being, he was merely a '*sleeper*' in the facility and nothing more. Also, part of the delay with the process moving forward was that Montell, wanted to hire a lawyer to represent him in the matter, and continuously refused a court appointed lawyer that the judicial system had in place for detainees who couldn't afford an attorney. This wasn't the situation for Montell. He had his mother and sister on the job looking for him a damn good lawyer to represent him on the case as a whole, and was granted a 30-day continuance by the judge there in Philly, so to find a lawyer for this purpose.

Throughout one of the phone calls that he had with his mother, she made him aware that indeed, a lawyer has been paid for to defend him as a whole, and should be there soon to visit with him. This was all Tamron's doing. She had Montell's Mother swear to God for her, that she wouldn't utter not a word to Montell, about them having contact with each other, and not a word about her (Tamron) actually being the one to put up the legal fees to have him thoroughly represented by a lawyer, her cousin. The mother agreed.

For the initial phone call that was had by the two—Tamron and Land—up to the day of the first attorney-client meeting between Landy and Montell, she was sure to file all

167

the necessary paperwork to notify the prosecution team and the court in Georgia, that she was now the attorney of record.

The day was in the middle of the week—'Hump day'—when Tamron made the drive to Philly from NYC. Montell was escorted out of the holding area of the jail to the designated visiting room to meet the awaiting lawyer of his who he knew nothing about. He jarred his head at the sight of Landy as he was taken through the doorway of the room. Montell was then handcuffed to the table that was itself firmly bolted to the floor. The guard then exited the room, leaving the two to proceed with their privileged conversation.

Montell, still stunned to see and now know that Landy, was a lawyer, continued to stand and look at her in awe. He finally spoke out. "Landy! What in the world!"

"And hello to you as well, Montell. Nice to see you again as well," she let out with a smile. "And who were you expecting, some fast talking, gum chewing, well-dressed white man with a briefcase, who might also be looking the part, but definitely no where near intent on playing the part, of representing you sincerely, with the type of charges you're facing down in Georgia. Now were you?"

They shook hands at this point.

Montell responded," No! I wasn't. But I *was* under the impression that my mom was gonna hire one of the top black male lawyers outta Atlanta. Or, either my homie Jamie would've. But... I got you. Which is cool too. And I'm assuming that Tamron sent you my way, right?"

"That's right."

"And since when the hell did you become a lawyer?"

"Throughout the time that you was away. When I graduated law school—Columbia University—I moved back home to practice law there for maybe six years. Then, a chance happen opportunity was offered by one of my sorority sisters who I went to law school with, I returned to

NYC and joined the law firm that her family owns. So... here I am," she related.

"And how you found out about the situation I'm in now?"

"I got a phone call from Tamron. So... In the words of Ms. Patti LaBelle, *'somebody loves you, baby!'*" she let out with a smile.

"Gotcha! I'm understanding now. But what all did Tamron mention to you?"

"She mentioned everything that I needed to know. Nothing more. Nothing less."

"Good! But from me to you... You do know that I ain't guilty of none of this shit that they accusing me of, don't you?"

"It's not necessary to try and convince you're innocent, Montell. I'm a criminal defense lawyer. My job is to get you the best possible outcome of the case. That's it."

"I just felt the need to say that so to eliminate any form of guilty that may enter into your mind and potentially have you not represent me to the best of your abilities. I know that a lawyer may not be so enthusiastic to represent a client that they know is guilty of the type of charges that I'm up against. That's why I said that."

"That's understandable. And I would've thought that it was pretty obvious by now, that neither Tamron nor me, believe that you did something like that. I was faced with a choice when I got the call from her. To either be your lawyer or not be so. I'm here. So that speaks for itself."

"It goddamn sure does. But let's go ahead and get do to the *nitty-gritty* about this. *When* will I be sent back to Georgia?"

"It'll be soon. But we could speed up the process, if you were to go ahead and sign a waiver." This was a suggestion in her own way. "The extradition hearing is nothing but a matter concerning the identity of the accused. And from the looks of things, you *are* who they say that you *are*. What's to dispute?"

"Right. Nothing really. But the GBI investigator—"

"Blake Gabbert," Landy interjected, upon flipping through the pages of her notepad.

"Yeah, that's his name. He said something to the effect about my identity being proven already through DNA if my blood."

"That's true," she replied, still reading from her notes. She spoke out again," and I would assume that the shooting incident you were involved in, is totally unrelated to the charges you now face, right?"

"Totally unrelated. How about I was shot and damn near killed behind a beef I ain't know nothing about, and didn't have nothing to do with."

"Lucky you is all I can say to that. But anyway, I have to ask this for legal purposes. Are you in agreement with me being the lawyer on your case moving forward? This has to be established before I officially file the '*Entry Of Appearance*' form."

"Yes ... I am. And I'm familiar with the process myself. I acquired a law degree while I was doing fed time," he said, making her aware of his understanding.

"Well good. That makes things a whole lot easier for me by not having to explain everything. In laymen terms at that. Woo!" she let loose with a chuckle.

"I'm sure you happy about that."

She winked at him before responding. "You better know that I am. The process is always a smooth ride anytime that I'm defending a client against criminal charges. Some learning of the law by a client is always good."

"I bet it is. But anyway. If anything ... What would you advise me to do?"

"Sign the waiver here," she said and placed the document on the table in front of him. She then handed him a blue fountain pen to sign with.

He did so. "There. Now what?"

"Now what, is that we wait. And more than likely, you'll be transported back to Georgia by the US Marshals. They're in charge of all transports across state lines. And once you're booked in the Hall County Jail there, I'll meet with you again, and we can proceed from that point."

"No doubt. I'm good with that. But before you go, I gotta ask you, Landy."

"I'm your attorney now. Ask me whatever it is that you want to."

"How much is Tamron paying you to represent me on this case?"

"A lot! And the retainer fee was paid in full already."

"More than $200k or less than?"

Montell called himself indirectly fact-checking the money status of Tamron, to know how heavy in the dope dealing business was she still, or, the lack thereof. He wanted to know how advanced was she now.

"More. Far more. Especially for those two big boy charges we gotta go up against. And the victim was a *'white girl'* at that! It wasn't gonna be no *'family friendly discounts'* on this one. I can tell you that much right now."

So, Tamron got rid of all the dope we had, paid off Pete, and probably kept things rolling like that I see.

Landy had more to say. "So, if anything, consider yourself blessed and fortunate to have a woman in your life like her. Because she loves you. Probably more than you'll ever know," she stated.

"Well, I do at least need a phone number to reach her, so I can call and tell her thanks. Wouldn't you agree?"

Landy then lifted the receiver to the phone that was there in the conference room where they were. She requested a line to dial out. One was provided. As she read the phone number from her notepad with one hand she punch in the digits with the other.

Tamron answered, "Hello!"

"Hey! It's me, Landy."

"Oh! Hey, Landy. How's everything going with you and Montell? And is this one of your other phone numbers?"

"No! It's not. And everything is going good with me and my new client, Montell. Actually, I'm at the County Jail in Philadelphia now visiting with him. He's right here with me. I'm on one of the facility phones in the lawyer's room. He can hear you."

"Hi, Tamron," Montell let out.

At the sound of his voice, a rush of affectionate energy shit throughout her body. They hadn't communicated in a while now, so just to hear from him and know that he was safe now and out of harms way of any more danger, brought about a strong sense of relief for her. He was fortunate to still be alive.

"Hello, Montell! I'm glad to know you okay. I heard about what happened," she expressed with a sincere heart.

"Yeah, I'm good. Thank God for this. And Landy told me it was you that hired her to help me fight this case. So, thank you for everything. And I'm assuming that you took care of the business we had going on?"

"I did. But now ain't the time and where you at ain't the place, to be talking about any of that. You needed a lawyer. I came through for you. Period."

"That's what's up. But I got one more thing to ask you before I let you go."

"Shoot."

"I wanna be able to keep in touch with you. Is it cool for Landy to give me your number?"

"Eventually, I'll be sure to get one of my numbers to you. Just be patient until you're finally transported back to Georgia for all that. And who knows, I just may pay you a visit when you're here. Just be cool."

"I'll do that. And I love you too, Tamron. Don't ever forget that." He was sure to let her at least hear him say this, if not but to express a form of appreciation towards her.

"Well, I know it ain't necessary to say the same thing back to you when in fact, I'm showing and providing it to you," she came back with. "But to at least satisfy you and your ego as a man ... I love you too, Montell. Now I gotta go. And you take care, okay."

"You do the same," he lastly said.

The call came to an end.

Landy spoke up again, "So you good now, right?"

"Oh yeah! You better know I am."

Epilogue

Meanwhile...

Eric and Joleena were down in Georgia themselves and visiting with his family. He was eager to introduce her to them all and make the fact known that he and Verena were no longer together, and that he'd moved on to someone younger and better.

The two were together with Eric's twin sister, Nasha. They were enjoying a day out and about in ATL. Their first stop was at the Lenox Square Mall. Eric and Joleena loved shopping for sneaker. He was obsessed with Air Jordan's and so was she. They often bought matching pairs. The same selection was picked up this day. But opposite the J's, Joleena racked up on several pairs of casual shoes too, the Vans, the K-Swiss, the Reebok Classics, and the Filas

When they left the mall, they went out to have a meal and a few rounds of cocktails. Eric dropped off Joleena from that point at the hotel suite they were staying so she could rest up for the night on the town they were intent on having. He and Nasha had really serious things to talk about and they needed the privacy to do so. They took the ride back to their mother's house. It had been a minute since Eric had been home and able to see his mother physically, with him being away up north for the past couple of years. But throughout the ride, the urgent conversation begun between him and his sibling.

Nasha initiated. "Bruh. We may get a few problems on our hands brewing behind that Keno shit," she stated. It was a warning of what could potentially come.

"What the fuck! That shit was almost three years ago. It should've been dead by now."

"You would think. But it ain't. And how about Zakeya's ass ... is the one that's now keeping it from dying."

"How's that?"

"The little bitch done became too muthafuckin' much for me to handle now. And not only that. She's closer to Keno's daughter now than they have ever been."

"How the fuck did this come to happen, the two of them getting close like this?"

"You know, before we took that bitch-ass nigga out that night, Zakeya and Kelly, had already been close together for the three years or so me and Keno was fucking around with each other. They right there around the same age, only Kelly is two months older. They eighteen. And just graduated this past May."

"So basically, they both seem to have a lot of questions now about what probably happened to dude?"

"That's about the sound of it. But more than likely, Kelly putting out the same questions that they family probably asking to include her own questions. And not just that. How 'bout, the muthafuckin' feds, pushed up on me at my job with a few questions of their own, too!"

"The muthafuckin' feds!"

"The muthafuckin' feds, bruh! They said something about after so long, with a person being on the Missing Persons list, that they got a duty to get involved. It's just been a lot going on behind that shit. And they say they been had Keno under investigation for the longest. He was named in their indictment, and the need to track him down so they can lock him up."

"So, they don't know if or not the nigga dead or alive, huh?"

"Nope! And this was why I needed you to fly home for us to talk in person about everything. Not over the phone. Because I'm pretty fuckin' convinced now, that if they were investigating him, and we had been fuckin' around for as long as we had, that they was investigating me too! So, the phones we been using, probably been tapped."

"—And we been talking over the phone like crazy about shit for the longest ... What the fuck! It ain't no telling what they know now it what they waiting to do about what all they know."

"It's something else I gotta tell you too, bruh."

"What's that?"

"They asked me about you too."

"*Humph!*" he scoffed. "What they wanted to know?"

"They wanted to know how long you been living in New Jersey? Did you give me the money to buy the house in Marietta I got? Did you give momma the money to buy her house? Shit about money moves, basically."

"It sounds like they busy tryna to dot '*i's*' and cross '*t's* on something."

"That could be true too. But that crazy ass woman you got kids by ... maybe she called them on you about something?"

"That could be true too. Because she did threaten me with an ultimatum one time before. And the bitch swore to God that if I left her, I would have hell to pay, so."

"And the feds probably bust tryna connect the dots on that with the shit about Keno still in the air."

"That too. But Keno ass, is *gone* bye-bye! Forever! That pussy-ass nigga ain't gonna ever come back!"

"Except as a muthafuckin' ghost, maybe, to haunt us."

"But look ... you sure Zakeya ain't got no idea about what happened to that nigga?"

"She don't know. Only still pissed off at me for forcing her to have that abortion back then. But time and time again, I done told her that the shit she was doing with Keno, it was wrong. That bitch-ass nigga had brainwashed my daughter, bruh!"

"Damn! That's some fucked up shit, there. And I was hoping that when we killed that nigga, that everything died with him. It didn't. Now all we gotta do is sit tight and wait to see what's gonna go on with the feds. And you ... you gotta be sure that Zakeya not talking too much about it no more, the situation that went on with her and dude."

"I think she probably done already said something to Kelly about the abortion, but didn't go so far as to say who she's pregnant by though."

"If anything, how could she be so brave as to tell *Kelly,* that she was pregnant by her Daddy ... her own *momma's* boyfriend?"

"You right, she can't. But I'mma be sure to have a woman-to-woman conversation with her, so that I'll know exactly what she could be running her mouth about."

"Yeah, you do that. And once it happens, then *we'll* know for certain."

They switch up the subject and begun to talk about other things that they need to catch up on as well.

No sooner than changing topics, they fought themes now pulled I to the house of their mother. She was anticipating Eric's return, because there was something that she'd saw on the news to catch her attention. When Eric walked through the front door, the mother immediately informed him on what she saw.

"Eric," she let out. "What in the world kinda trouble has your friend Montell got himself in? They got that boy all over the news."

"I don't know that nigga like that no more, momma. He ain't my friend. And whatever it is that they done locked him up for, I believe he done it. I definitely do believe that much about him."

"He's got a mess on his hands to deal with. And when y'all fell out with each other?" she asked.

"We ain't been cool for awhile now, momma."

"Well, what happened?"

"It's a long story, momma. A long story."

"Behind a woman or about some money?"

"Both."

"Well ... I just thought that I'd let you know."

"Thank you."

They begin talking about other things at this point. Mostly about his uncle Charles, his mothers brother, having a worker of his that got arrested and potentially snitching, and a tip about a possible federal indictment coming down on him as a result of the worker having a loose tongue.

***

Several Days Later...

The feds had gotten a tip from an anonymous caller about a mortician by the name of Charles Mickens. He was someone that also held a major role in a drug network that supplied hundreds of kilos of narcotics products to the underworld of Atlanta. The snitch made the claim to them that Charles and the operation he ran, utilized the hearse vehicles Charles owned, to not only transport corpses from Miami Florida as decoy, but large caches of heroin as well, to the designated location of the funeral home, in zone one West side of Atlanta, in *The Bluff*.

Apparently, the male doing the talking to the feds, worked for Charles at one point. His job was to get rid of the product. A dispute broke out between the two that couldn't be fixed. It wouldn't involve anything violent or bring about death even, so long as either side was willing to walk away with the fact of taking a loss financially in the process. This was the rat who had to go on with the loss, after not long before having plenty. His was taken for just over a million dollars in cash and was so pissed off about it. Something had to be done, he concluded. This resulted in the feds being contacted. Precise details were told about how exactly Charles's operation was ran. A wiretap warrant was issued to track and record Charles' phones and him personally.

No soon after more information was gained, the feds followed one of Charles's drivers all the way down to Miami. He was allowed the leeway to pick up his load of kilos, 75 total, and was busted the very moment he recrossed back into Georgia. It was early in the a.m. The forty-eight-year-old carrier himself, wasted no time giving up Charles too. Now the feds had a confidential informant in their custody.

"You're in a whole lot of trouble here, Ellis. A *whole* lot of trouble, buddy!" stated special agent Alfonso Crumpton, of the field office of the FBI located in Valdosta Georgia. The arrest was a joint venture by both field offices, the one in Atlanta, and the one in South Georgia. Crumpton worked in the North Georgia one. He had the C.I. Ellis brought back to the city.

The special agent spoke out yet again," Not only was you transporting a *dead body* to and from Miami ... Your ass was loaded with thirty guns and seventy-five kilos of fucking fentanyl laced heroin, wasn't you. And with your record of aggravated assault and possession of a firearm that you served five years in prison for, according to the sentencing guidelines I'm now having a look at here, (he held up the laminated chart) lets see how much time you facing here, shall we. Hmm ... twenty years ... thirty years ... forty years ... Shit, this damn thing still going up on you, but buddy. So ... if you know like I know, won't you do yourself a favor and save your own ass by giving up the motherfucker that you work for, won't you? The motherfucker you've been hauling all this shit for these many years. That'll be the funeral home director, Charles Mickens. And so you'll know, we followed you all the way down to Miami, allowed you time to load up and do your thing, and then drive all the way back across state lines here, so we could nail hours ass to the cross right here in our jurisdiction. We already knew everything well ahead of time. Now all we need is for you to corroborate what we got by being a compliant witness to help your own self," said the dark complexioned bald-headed, clean-shaven veteran agent.

The detainee Ellis looked up and held a stern gaze into the eyes of Crumpton. He said to him, "If I tell you everything you wanna know about who it is you wanna know about, how serious are you willing to be about helping me outta this here situation I done found myself in? Because it ain't no way that I'm gonna let myself go to prison for the rest of my damn life, behind some shit that don't even belong to me! It ain't no muthafuckin' way! I'm forty-eight, and don't feel like I got that much more time left on this here side of the grave. So ... with that having been said ... what the fuck you wanna know? I'm willing to tell y'all *everything.* And when I say everything, that's what the fuck I mean ... *everything!*"

"You see ... now ... now you speaking my kinda language here. It's called '*cooperation,*'" Crumpton let out, now possessing a huge smile about his face, with those black-ass lips of his like Whoopi Goldberg.

Ellis left no stone not turned with what all he told to the feds about Charles. The agents were issued warrants immediately to raid the home and businesses of the Kingpin mortician, Charles. His reign in the Atlanta underworld and influence in society, was about to come to a crushing end. And it was all behind him helping his cutthroat and grimy nephew Eric and his twin sister Nasha, get rid of a body when they put down Keno.

My-my-my, how the tables have turned. Karma is always a vicious bill collector. And when she comes to see you, she takes no shorts. Only full payments.

To Be Continued...

ABOUT THE AUTHOR

PRINCE, is a writer of gritty, raw, dark, and suspenseful contemporary urban/street crime fiction. The works of his, embody American society and African-American culture, as is, in the way that it is. Nothing less. Nothing more. The characters he creates, are realistic in nature, in all of their wiles and ways. The style of writing Prince has developed, speaks for itself. You're drawn in the more and more you read, until you're locked there; with one way in and no way out. In a word to describe his skills within the craft: it's **LETHAL.**

Prince, vehemently declares at every opportunity that *"WRITING, IS HIS ONLY SALVATION!"* He stands firmly on business with this.

The works he's released thus far in addition to this, is the popular **BLOODLINE OF A SAVAGE** series (three installments to date); **THESE VICIOUS STREETS** series (three installments to date); and **RELENTLESS GOON** series; (three installments to date) to name a few. More captivating stories are on the way.

Prince is currently hard at work on his next installment of the story you've just read. Look forward to new releases from him soon. He highly encourages feedback and engaging conversation about his books in general and the writing industry as a whole. You may contact him at the following:

PRINCE A. TAUHID #952058
MACON STATE PRISON
P.O. BOX 426
OGLETHORPE, GEORGIA 31068
iamprinceforever3000@gmail.com

The Pen Is Mightier Than The Pistol
EMBRACE WRITING!

Lock Down Publications and Ca$h Presents
Assisted Publishing Packages

Due to an increase in the price of services we have increased our prices. The prices below reflect the price increase as of 11/1/24.

BASIC PACKAGE	UPGRADED PACKAGE
$699	$1000
Editing	Typing
Cover Design	Editing
Formatting	Cover Design
	Formatting
	Upload eBooks to Amazon
	Upload Paperback to Amazon
ADVANCE PACKAGE	**LDP SUPREME PACKAGE**
$1,400	$1,700
Typing	Typing
Editing (line editing/content)	Editing (line editing/content)
Cover Design	Cover Design
Formatting	Formatting
Copyright Registration	Copyright Registration
Proofreading	Proofreading
Upload eBooks to Amazon	Set up Amazon Account
Upload Paperback to Amazon	Upload eBooks to Amazon
	Upload Paperback to Amazon
	Advertise on LDP's Amazon and Facebook Page

***

Other services available upon request.
Additional charges may apply

Lock Down Publications
P.O. Box 944
Stockbridge, GA 30281-9998
Phone: 470 303-9761
Email: lockdownpublications@gmail.com

Submission Guideline

Submit the first three chapters of your completed manuscript to ldpsubmissions@gmail.com. In the subject line add **Your Book's Title**. The manuscript must be in a Word Doc file and sent as an attachment. Document should be in Times New Roman, double spaced, and in size 12 font. Also, provide your synopsis and full contact information. If sending multiple submissions, they must each be in a separate email.

Have a story but no way to send it electronically? You can still submit to LDP/Ca$h Presents. Send in the first three chapters, written or typed, of your completed manuscript to:

LDP: Submissions Dept
P.O. Box 944
Stockbridge, GA 30281-9998

DO NOT send original manuscript. Must be a duplicate. Provide your synopsis and a cover letter containing your full contact information.

Thanks for considering LDP and Ca$h Presents.

NEW RELEASES

BLOODLINE OF A SAVAGE 1-3
THESE VICIOUS STREETS 1-3
RELENTLESS GOON 1-3
BY PRINCE A. TAUHID

THE BUTTERFLY MAFIA 1-3
BY FUMIYA PAYNE

A THUG'S STREET PRINCESS 1&2
BY MEESHA

CITY OF SMOKE 3
BY MOLOTTI

GET IT IN SLUGS 1 &2
BY B. STALL

STANDING ON HER BUSINESS 1&2
BY DG SANTANA

STEPPERS 1,2&3
THE REAL BADDIES OF CHI-RAQ
BY KING RIO

THE LANE 1&2
BY KEN-KEN SPENCE

THUG OF SPADES 1&2
LOVE IN THE TRENCHES 2
CORNER BOYS
BY COREY ROBINSON

TIL DEATH 3
BY ARYANNA

THE DIRTY SIDE OF MONEY 3 | PRINCE

THE BIRTH OF A GANGSTER 4
BY DELMONT PLAYER

PRODUCT OF THE STREETS 1-3
BY DEMOND "MONEY" ANDERSON

NO TIME FOR ERROR
BY KEESE

MONEY HUNGRY DEMONS 1-2
BY TRANAY ADAMS

HUB CITY MENACE 1-3
BY J. WHITE

A THUGGISH PASSION 1&2
LAND OF DA HOOLIGANZ 1-4
KILLAZ ON STANDBY 1&2
BY IRA B.

FO'EVA ROLLIN 1&2
BY ASSA RAYMOND BAKER

THE LEVEL UP 1&3
BY LUXURY KING

Coming Soon from Lock Down Publications/Ca$h Presents

IF YOU CROSS ME ONCE 6
ANGEL V
By Anthony Fields

A THUGS STREET PRINCESS 3
By Meesha

CORNER BOYS 2
By Corey Robinson

THA TAKEOVER
By Keith Chandler

BETRAYAL OF A G 2
By Ray Vinci

SAVAGE FAMILY EMPIRE 1&2
SOULLESS GOON 1,2&3
THE DIRTY SIDE OF MONEY 1,2&3
By Prince

FOR MY ENEMY'S SAKE
AMBITIONS OF A SLIDER
FRESH OFF DA PORCH
By IRA B.

THE TRUCKLOAD 1-4
TIPPIN' THE SCALES 1-3
BAD BITCHES WIT GUNZ 3
PROBLEM SOLVED 2
By Christopher "Diesel" Hornezes

Available Now

RESTRAINING ORDER 1 & 2
By **CA$H & Coffee**

LOVE KNOWS NO BOUNDARIES 1-3
By **Coffee**

RAISED AS A GOON I, II, III & IV
BRED BY THE SLUMS I, II, III
BLAST FOR ME I & II
ROTTEN TO THE CORE I II III
A BRONX TALE I, II, III
DUFFLE BAG CARTEL I II III IV V VI
HEARTLESS GOON I II III IV V
A SAVAGE DOPEBOY I II
DRUG LORDS I II III
CUTTHROAT MAFIA I II
KING OF THE TRENCHES
By **Ghost**

LAY IT DOWN I & II
LAST OF A DYING BREED I II
BLOOD STAINS OF A SHOTTA I & II III
By **Jamaica**

LOYAL TO THE GAME I II III
LIFE OF SIN I, II III
By **TJ & Jelissa**

IF LOVING HIM IS WRONG...I & II
LOVE ME EVEN WHEN IT HURTS I II III
By **Jelissa**

PUSH IT TO THE LIMIT
By **Bre' Hayes**

BLOODY COMMAS I & II
SKI MASK CARTEL I, II & III
KING OF NEW YORK I II, III IV V
RISE TO POWER I II III
COKE KINGS I II III IV V
BORN HEARTLESS I II III IV
KING OF THE TRAP I II
By **T.J. Edwards**

WHEN THE STREETS CLAP BACK I & II III
THE HEART OF A SAVAGE I II III IV
MONEY MAFIA I II
LOYAL TO THE SOIL I II III
By **Jibril Williams**

A DISTINGUISHED THUG STOLE MY HEART I II & III
LOVE SHOULDN'T HURT I II III IV
RENEGADE BOYS 1-4
PAID IN KARMA 1-3
SAVAGE STORMS 1-3
AN UNFORESEEN LOVE 1-3
BABY, I'M WINTERTIME COLD 1-3
A THUG'S STREET PRINCESS 1&2
By **Meesha**

A GANGSTER'S CODE 1-3
A GANGSTER'S SYN 1-3
THE SAVAGE LIFE 1-3
CHAINED TO THE STREETS 1-3
BLOOD ON THE MONEY 1-3
A GANGSTA'S PAIN 1-3
BEAUTIFUL LIES AND UGLY TRUTHS
CHURCH IN THESE STREETS
By **J-Blunt**

CUM FOR ME 1-8
An LDP Erotica Collaboration

THE DIRTY SIDE OF MONEY 3 | PRINCE

BLOOD OF A BOSS 1-5
SHADOWS OF THE GAME
TRAP BASTARD
By **Askari**

THE STREETS BLEED MURDER 1-3
THE HEART OF A GANGSTA 1-3
By **Jerry Jackson**

WHEN A GOOD GIRL GOES BAD
By **Adrienne**

THE COST OF LOYALTY 1-3
By **Kweli**

BRIDE OF A HUSTLA 1-3
THE FETTI GIRLS 1-3
CORRUPTED BY A GANGSTA 1-4
BLINDED BY HIS LOVE
THE PRICE YOU PAY FOR LOVE 1-3
DOPE GIRL MAGIC 1-3
By **Destiny Skai**

A KINGPIN'S AMBITION
A KINGPIN'S AMBITION II
I MURDER FOR THE DOUGH
By **Ambitious**

TRUE SAVAGE 1-7
DOPE BOY MAGIC 1-3
MIDNIGHT CARTEL 1-3
CITY OF KINGZ 1&2
NIGHTMARE ON SILENT AVE
THE PLUG OF LIL MEXICO 1&2
CLASSIC CITY
By **Chris Green**

A GANGSTER'S REVENGE 1-4
THE BOSS MAN'S DAUGHTERS 1-5
A SAVAGE LOVE 1&2
BAE BELONGS TO ME 1&2
A HUSTLER'S DECEIT 1-3
WHAT BAD BITCHES DO 1-3
SOUL OF A MONSTER 1-3
KILL ZONE
A DOPE BOY'S QUEEN 1-3
TIL DEATH 1-3
IMMA DIE BOUT MINE 1-6
DYING FOR LIKES
By **Aryanna**

A DOPEBOY'S PRAYER
By **Eddie "Wolf" Lee**

THE KING CARTEL 1-3
By **Frank Gresham**

THESE NIGGAS AIN'T LOYAL 1-3
By **Nikki Tee**

GANGSTA SHYT 1-3
By **CATO**

THE ULTIMATE BETRAYAL
By **Phoenix**

BOSS'N UP 1-3
By **Royal Nicole**

I LOVE YOU TO DEATH
By **Destiny J**

I RIDE FOR MY HITTA
I STILL RIDE FOR MY HITTA
By **Misty Holt**

LOVE & CHASIN' PAPER
By **Qay Crockett**

TO DIE IN VAIN
SINS OF A HUSTLA
By **ASAD**

BROOKLYN HUSTLAZ
By **Boogsy Morina**

BROOKLYN ON LOCK 1 & 2
By **Sonovia**

GANGSTA CITY
By **Teddy Duke**

A DRUG KING AND HIS DIAMOND 1-3
A DOPEMAN'S RICHES
HER MAN, MINE'S TOO 1&2
CASH MONEY HO'S
THE WIFEY I USED TO BE 1&2
PRETTY GIRLS DO NASTY THINGS
By **Nicole Goosby**

LIPSTICK KILLAH 1-3
CRIME OF PASSION 1-3
FRIEND OR FOE 1-3
By **Mimi**

TRAPHOUSE KING 1-3
KINGPIN KILLAZ 1-3
STREET KINGS 1&2
PAID IN BLOOD 1&2
CARTEL KILLAZ 1-3
DOPE GODS 1&2
By **Hood Rich**

THE STREETS ARE CALLING
By **Duquie Wilson**

STEADY MOBBN' 1-3
THE STREETS STAINED MY SOUL 1-3
By **Marcellus Allen**

WHO SHOT YA 1-3
SON OF A DOPE FIEND 1-4
HEAVEN GOT A GHETTO 1&2
SKI MASK MONEY 1&2
By **Renta**

GORILLAZ IN THE BAY 1-4
TEARS OF A GANGSTA 1/&2
3X KRAZY 1&2
STRAIGHT BEAST MODE 1&2
By **DE'KARI**

TRIGGADALE 1-3
MURDA WAS THE CASE 1-3
By **Elijah R. Freeman**

SLAUGHTER GANG 1-3
RUTHLESS HEART 1-3
By **Willie Slaughter**

GOD BLESS THE TRAPPERS 1-3
THESE SCANDALOUS STREETS 1-3
FEAR MY GANGSTA 1-5
THESE STREETS DON'T LOVE NOBODY 1-2
BURY ME A G 1-5
A GANGSTA'S EMPIRE 1-4
THE DOPEMAN'S BODYGAURD 1&2
THE REALEST KILLAZ 1-3
THE LAST OF THE OGS 1-3
By **Tranay Adams**

MARRIED TO A BOSS 1-3
By **Destiny Skai & Chris Green**

KINGZ OF THE GAME 1-7
CRIME BOSS 1-4
By **Playa Ray**

FUK SHYT
By **Blakk Diamond**

DON'T F#CK WITH MY HEART 1&2
By **Linnea**

ADDICTED TO THE DRAMA 1-3
IN THE ARM OF HIS BOSS
By **Jamila**

LOYALTY AIN'T PROMISED 1&2
By **Keith Williams**

YAYO 1-4
A SHOOTER'S AMBITION 1&2
BRED IN THE GAME
By **S. Allen**

TRAP GOD 1-3
RICH $AVAGE 1-3
MONEY IN THE GRAVE 1-3
CARTEL MONEY 1&2
By **Martell Troublesome Bolden**

FOREVER GANGSTA 1&2
GLOCKS ON SATIN SHEETS 1&2
By **Adrian Dulan**

TOE TAGZ 1-4
LEVELS TO THIS SHYT 1&2
IT'S JUST ME AND YOU
By **Ah'Million**

KINGPIN DREAMS 1-3
RAN OFF ON DA PLUG
By **Paper Boi Rari**

THE STREETS MADE ME 1-3
By **Larry D. Wright**

CONFESSIONS OF A GANGSTA 1-4
CONFESSIONS OF A JACKBOY 1-3
CONFESSIONS OF A HITMAN
CONFESSIONS OF A DOPE BOY
By **Nicholas Lock**

I'M NOTHING WITHOUT HIS LOVE
SINS OF A THUG
TO THE THUG I LOVED BEFORE
A GANGSTA SAVED XMAS
IN A HUSTLER I TRUST
By **Monet Dragun**

QUIET MONEY 1-3
THUG LIFE 1-3
EXTENDED CLIP 1&2
A GANGSTA'S PARADISE
By **Trai'Quan**

CAUGHT UP IN THE LIFE 1-3
THE STREETS NEVER LET GO 1-3
By **Robert Baptiste**

NEW TO THE GAME 1-3
MONEY, MURDER & MEMORIES 1-3
By **Malik D. Rice**

CREAM 2-3
THE STREETS WILL TALK
By **Yolanda Moore**

THE DIRTY SIDE OF MONEY 3 | PRINCE

THE STREETS WILL NEVER CLOSE 1-3
By **K'ajji**

LIFE OF A SAVAGE 1-4
A GANGSTA'S QUR'AN 1-4
MURDA SEASON 1-3
GANGLAND CARTEL 1-3
CHI'RAQ GANGSTAS 1-4
KILLERS ON ELM STREET 1-3
JACK BOYZ N DA BRONX 1-3
A DOPEBOY'S DREAM 1-3
JACK BOYS VS DOPE BOYS 1-3
COKE GIRLZ
COKE BOYS
SOSA GANG 1&2
BRONX SAVAGES
BODYMORE KINGPINS
BLOOD OF A GOON
By **Romell Tukes**

CONCRETE KILLA 1-3
VICIOUS LOYALTY 1-3
BLOODY MONEY BAGS
By **Kingpen**

THE ULTIMATE SACRIFICE 1-6
KHADIFI
IF YOU CROSS ME ONCE 1-3
ANGEL 1-4
IN THE BLINK OF AN EYE
By **Anthony Fields**

THE LIFE OF A HOOD STAR
By **Ca$h & Rashia Wilson**

NIGHTMARES OF A HUSTLA 1-3
BLOOD AND GAMES 1&2
By **King Dream**

GHOST MOB
By **Stilloan Robinson**

HARD AND RUTHLESS 1&2
MOB TOWN 251
THE BILLIONAIRE BENTLEYS 1-3
REAL G'S MOVE IN SILENCE
By **Von Diesel**

MOB TIES 1-7
SOUL OF A HUSTLER, HEART OF A KILLER 1-3
GORILLAZ IN THE TRENCHES
OOPS CRY TOO 1&2
THE DAUGHTER OF A CARTEL BOSS
By **SayNoMore**

BODYMORE MURDERLAND 1-3
THE BIRTH OF A GANGSTER 1-4
By **Delmont Player**

FOR THE LOVE OF A BOSS 1&2
By **C. D. Blue**

KILLA KOUNTY 1-5
TENDER
By **Khufu**

MOBBED UP 1-4
THE BRICK MAN 1-5
THE COCAINE PRINCESS 1-10
STEPPERS 1-3
SUPER GREMLIN 1-4
A GANGSTA'S SON
By **King Rio**

MONEY GAME 1&2
By **Smoove Dolla**

A GANGSTA'S KARMA 1-5
By **FLAME**

KING OF THE TRENCHES 1-3
By **GHOST & TRANAY ADAMS**

BAD BITCHES WIT GUNZ 1&2
PROBLEM SOLVED
By **"Christopher Diesel" Hornezes**

QUEEN OF THE ZOO 1&2
By **Black Migo**

GRIMEY WAYS 1-3
BETRAYAL OF A G
By **Ray Vinci**

XMAS WITH AN ATL SHOOTER
By **Ca$h & Destiny Skai**

KING KILLA 1&2
By **Vincent "Vitto" Holloway**

BETRAYAL OF A THUG 1&2
By **Fre$h**

COUNTDOWN OF A KILLA 1&2
SEX, MURDER AND GOD 1&2
GUNS DOWN, BOTTOMS UP 1&2
By Lo-Life

THE MURDER QUEENS 1-7
By **Michael Gallon**

FOR THE LOVE OF BLOOD 1-4
By **Jamel Mitchell**

THE DIRTY SIDE OF MONEY 3 | PRINCE

HOOD CONSIGLIERE 1&2
NO TIME FOR ERROR
By **Keese**

PROTÉGÉ OF A LEGEND 1,2&3
LOVE IN THE TRENCHES 1&2
By **Corey Robinson**

THE PLUG'S RUTHLESS DAUGHTER 1&2
By **Tony Daniels**

BORN IN THE GRAVE 1-3
CRIME PAYS
By **Self Made Tay**

MOAN IN MY MOUTH
By **XTASY**

TORN BETWEEN A GANGSTER AND A GENTLEMAN
By **J-BLUNT & Miss Kim**

LOYALTY IS EVERYTHING 1-3
CITY OF SMOKE 1-3
By **Molotti**

HERE TODAY GONE TOMORROW 1&2
By **Fly Rock**

WOMEN LIE MEN LIE 1-4
FIFTY SHADES OF SNOW 1-3
STACK BEFORE YOU SPLURGE
GIRLS FALL LIKE DOMINOES
NAÏVE TO THE STREETS
By **ROY MILLIGAN**

PILLOW PRINCESS
By **S. Hawkins**

THE DIRTY SIDE OF MONEY 3 | PRINCE

THE BUTTERFLY MAFIA 1-3
SALUTE MY SAVAGERY 1&2
By **Fumiya Payne**

THE LANE 1&2
By Ken-Ken Spence

THE PUSSY TRAP 1-5
By **Nene Capri**

DIRTY DNA
By **Blaque**

SANCTIFIED AND HORNY
by **XTASY**

BOOKS BY LDP'S CEO, CA$H

TRUST IN NO MAN
TRUST IN NO MAN 2
TRUST IN NO MAN 3
BONDED BY BLOOD
SHORTY GOT A THUG
THUGS CRY
THUGS CRY 2
THUGS CRY 3
TRUST NO BITCH
TRUST NO BITCH 2
TRUST NO BITCH 3
TIL MY CASKET DROPS
RESTRAINING ORDER
RESTRAINING ORDER 2
IN LOVE WITH A CONVICT
LIFE OF A HOOD STAR
XMAS WITH AN ATL SHOOTER

www.ingramcontent.com/pod-product-compliance
Lightning Source LLC
Chambersburg PA
CBHW070757280626
47162CB00016B/1159

* 9 7 8 1 9 6 5 4 4 8 7 2 4 *